HOSTAGE TO LOVE

HOSTAGE TO LOVE

Helen McCabe

CHIVERS

British Library Cataloguing in Publication Data available

This Large Print edition published by BBC Audiobooks Ltd, Bath, 2007.
Published by arrangement with the Author.

U.K. Hardcover ISBN 978 1 405 64094 7
U.K. Softcover   ISBN 978 1 405 64095 4

Printed and bound in Great Britain by Antony Rowe Ltd., Chippenham,
Wiltshire

Dedication

To my dear neighbors, Barbara and Les

Chapter One

'Take it away!' Conor shouted, and the hard-baked terracotta earth disappeared at an alarming angle. Lucy gasped, losing her breath, as the chopper swooped upwards, its egg-beater blades whisking them up and whirling them off towards the humped black-raisin mountains.

'Flown in one before?' he questioned, swivelling in his seat, his dark eyes narrow against the sunlight, the tiniest hint of an amused smile teasing his lips. Even in that breathless moment, she couldn't fail to notice once more just how good-looking he was.

'What?' she shouted. Not used to headphones, she was having difficulty in hearing what he was saying over the noise of the engines.

'Have you flown in one before?'

'Flown? Of course I have.'

'In a chopper.' Conor lifted his eyebrows.

'Oh . . .' Lucy got her breath back now. He'd meant in a helicopter. 'No . . . no, I haven't,' she admitted. She fiddled with her earphones to cover her embarrassment at the misunderstanding. There was nothing she hated more than feeling at a disadvantage. Especially in front of someone as cool as he obviously thought he was. Ice-cool, in fact.

'Right. Enjoy the experience.' She bristled as he swung back, turning to the pilot and asking in Arabic, 'How long?'

'150 minutes ETA. Given the wind speed.' Then, immediately, the two men were engrossed in the flight instructions.'

Lucy squashed her rising resentment as she listened. It was a feeling she was rapidly having to get used to.

It doesn't matter about his attitude, she told herself as she had been doing ever since she arrived in the Middle East. However arrogant Conor Kendall might be, she was going to ignore it. Because, she needed to get Matt out.

She closed her eyes momentarily to calm herself. To convince herself what she wanted most in the world had begun, at last. Nothing else mattered, because she was now here in the Yemen, and somewhere, in those far distant humped black mountains, Matt was being held captive.

Conor had been detailed to find her brother's hiding place, and she was going to help. They needed each other.

She studied her companion, who was chatting away in Arabic with the pilot. She'd only been in the country forty-eight hours, but she'd already discovered when they found themselves alone together that Conor was hard going, even reticent. However, it seemed he had no problem conversing freely with his male companions.

At that moment, she enjoyed the opportunity to study his profile. Good-looking wasn't the word. Maybe it should have been stunning? Not entirely regular, but full of character from the resolute eyes, strong nose and cleft chin. She always found men, who were too handsome, were usually arrogant and self-centred once you got to know them. So far, she hadn't the opportunity to find about his regard for himself, but her assumption about his arrogance was already proving to be right . . . However, in spite of her first impression of his high-handedness, she found herself drawn to him, if only on account of his looks. She'd always been attracted to dark, handsome men.

She wondered if he let his hair grow, whether it would be curly. He was as dark-skinned as a Latin, but the sun had made it that way. His tan was the colour of teak-wood, and his strong cheekbones were high and smooth until her eyes detected the slightest hint of stubble. He was dark enough to be a two-shaves a day man.

As he talked to the pilot, his whole demeanour reeked of power and authority and that was what Lucy needed. Someone as strong as she, and maybe stronger. Determined and tough enough to get her brother out of the hands of the terrorists. According to the British Consul, Conor Kendall was the best man for the job. She

3

remembered the way the official looked, when he said 'If anyone can pull it off with Abdul, Miss Page, it's Kendall. I'm confident he will be able to rescue your brother.'

She prayed it was true, staring at her companion's broad back. She noticed how deep his tan plunged beneath the collar of his soft, sage-green shirt. As her eyes lingered on his neck, she wondered if he was as bronzed all over. It was a tantalizing thought, that produced a tiny throb of pleasure inside her.

His colour hadn't come from spending winters in London. In fact, she guessed he must have been living in hot climates for a very long time but, according to the Consul, Conor was based permanently in Whitehall. Which definitely seemed a bit odd.

She breathed in, tasting the dust on her tongue, lost in her thoughts. She continued to stare absently at his back, recalling just how long and how much persuasion it had taken, over so many weeks, for the powers-that-be to agree to search for Matt.

They kept on telling his family everything that could be done was being done, but Lucy continued to pester them, determined to set out on her own if she had to, a threat, which she hoped would persuade them to change their tactics.

She was counting on the fact the last thing the Foreign Office wanted, was another of their nationals being taken hostage. Whether she would actually have set out alone, was another matter.

Other factors counted, too. There had been no word from the tribesmen when Matt was first taken. In fact, Lucy and her mother got to the point of almost believing they would never see him again, when their luck turned and they were told his kidnappers had at last made firm contact with the British authorities.

It seemed the tribesmen wanted to negotiate, and, then, suddenly, the Foreign Office contacted her, offering a negotiator in the shape of Kendall. They also, very reluctantly, agreed to allow her to go along, but strictly at her own risk.

She was sure being who she was helped to sway their decision. It seemed her father's name and reputation still counted for something, but it was pointless thinking about her father, she told herself quickly and just as pointless to spend too much time worrying if the kidnappers' demands weren't met, it could be too late to rescue Matt.

To take her mind off such an awful possibility—her brother had to stay alive until they reached him—Lucy's thoughts returned to Conor, focusing on the back of his neck.

How did he get that scar? She'd noticed it straightaway. It was shaped like a cross. Stark white against the bronzed skin. If he'd grown his hair a bit longer, it wouldn't have shown, but she expected being a man, he didn't bother about things like that. She suddenly wanted to trace the scar with the tip of her finger, make him turn round and notice her properly, but she squashed the thought firmly. She was here to find Matt. Not to get together with Conor Kendall.

As he and the young Army pilot continued to talk shop, Lucy fantasized as to what he might have been involved in. Was the scar an old bullet wound? Or a knife cut? She frowned. Possibly an operation? Yet he looked too fit. It was for more interesting to imagine he'd been involved in something very exciting. Her eyes lingered on the breadth of his shoulders, willing him to turn in her direction. The magic worked.

He swung round again and she held his steady gaze for a moment, before lowering her eyes to the map he was holding in his hands.

'Do you want to know where we are, Miss Page?'

'Of course,' Lucy replied, feeling a trifle embarrassed at having been caught off guard. Teasing was all right, but it had to be on her terms. Trying to concentrate, she wiped the perspiration from her face but, all the time, the man's nearness was thrilling. Come on she told herself grimly. She had other and far more serious things to think about than spending her time sizing up a guy whose whole attitude proclaimed the fact he basically considered her a waste of space. His smooth

6

brown finger pointed down at the map. 'We're over the coastal plain. These low mountains give rise to peaks in the central massif of over ten thousand feet. Unfortunately, that's the direction in which we're heading.' Her concern must have showed on her face. 'Don't worry. We've an expert guide laid on,' he continued. 'We're meeting Khalid here.' He indicated the place on the map.

'I'm not worried,' she replied coolly, gazing at the indeterminate dot.

'Good.' Conor noted her dust-streaked face, flushed with heat and wondered how in the hell she was going to manage. There was no going back now.

He had been dead set against having to accept her company. He preferred to travel alone or, at least, with a hand-picked company of men and he told the bosses so. Moreover, travelling through the wild terrain of the Yemen was definitely not like going on an English picnic and, nowadays, of course, it was also bloody dangerous.

That thick blond hair, which looked good enough to touch, would soon be tangled with sweat and heat, bleached white by the fearsome sun as they made their way further south from Sana'a.

Yemen's capital city, Sana'a, was around eight thousand feet above sea level so, although the air was thin, the heat was at least bearable. They were now heading towards the southern mountains, and when their fairly comfortable helicopter ride to their rendezvous with Khalid was over, they would be trekking over broken, dissected terrain in punishing temperatures, which often exceeded thirty-eight degrees.

Conor saw far too many people in places where they shouldn't be, from the unprepared walkers in the snowy Scottish Highlands to pig-ignorant tourists in some dangerous foreign hot spots and, having made a balls up, it meant that much time and effort had to go into organising their rescue.

And, now, this girl, as well as her brother, was his responsibility. How would she cope? His first impression of Lucy Page was she was an extremely good-looking girl, who would have been better off staying in London where she belonged, and letting the proper authorities handle the case.

When he met her off the plane at Sana'a, she was wearing the required long-sleeved white cotton shirt and trousers, but her clothes had done nothing to hide the shape of her lissom figure.

She pushed back her dark-blond hair and stared up at him out of strangely light-blue eyes. 'I'm so pleased to meet you at last, Mr Kendall,' she said.

'Same here,' he replied. He felt slightly unnerved, which was not a feeling which he was used to. Mainly, because it was evident she assumed he would be able to free her brother and he wasn't sure he could fulfill her trust in him. There was a real possibility he would not be able to rescue Matt Page. That they might get killed trying.

As he took her warm, smooth hand, the thought of what she might have to face in the coming weeks turned his stomach over.

Then she tossed back her lovely mane again and asked, 'When do we leave for the mountains?' She was chock full of the enthusiasm he'd lost a long time ago. He knew it wouldn't be long before her girlish dream of him as a knight in shining armor dissolved. The useless waste of it all riled him.

'First things first, Dr. Page,' he snapped and he caught the blank surprise in her look.

'You can drop the "doctor,"' she snapped back, recovering herself. He liked that. She had self-control and she was not so self-important as to need her academic title. After that, he called her Miss.

That first impression set off warning bells in his head. He wanted to say: Get back on the plane. Go home to your family and your university job. Leave it to me to get your brother out safely. This place is no good for you. This country will change you. Just as it's done to me.

Evidently, Lucy Page's looks belied her will. From what he had learned about her so far, in the short time which they'd spent together, she

9

was as stubborn as her brother, but how about her stamina? He hoped to God they both had that. He shook his head imperceptibly.

If her brother had been less headstrong and more circumspect, and used the intelligence he most certainly possessed, he wouldn't have been in the wrong place at the wrong time.

He must have known what he did to that shrine was desecration. The result of such stupidity had been that Matt Page was taken hostage. The young academic was now in the hands of a gang of bloodthirsty, fanatical madmen, led by Abdul, one of the craziest of all.

It had been crass thoughtlessness on the boy's part. The repercussions of his actions had not only put his own life in danger, but everyone else's, including his sister's. This made Conor very angry. Especially since he was the one, who was ordered to rescue the lad.

He smiled ruefully to himself, as the calm words of the Koran slipped into his mind. He glanced down at the landscape whirling beneath. The earth is the carpet of God. His own world had never been like that. He wallowed too deep in the mud.

Little fields now gave way to featureless desert, interspersed by deep valleys from which rose the most amazing rock pinnacles, thrusting like needles out of the landscape.

He sat half-turned towards Lucy, motionless, staring down, but she could see he was not relaxed. He reminded her of some lithe and brooding animal. Always on guard. What was he thinking? What were his secrets? She would have given anything to know. She stared down too.

Her first impression of him had been rather different. He was not the earnest, bespectacled civil servant whom she had been expecting to meet.

What a dish, she thought to herself as she extended her hand and been rewarded by the briefest of handshakes.

He was about thirty, six foot four and good-looking in an interesting way, strong featured with short, dark hair. Not a perfect profile, but one full of character. Obviously intelligent and extremely fit. The kind of man she went for and, who, unfortunately, was very thin on the ground.

Briefly, she found herself thinking about Nick. He had been her boy friend, but she broke off with him before she came out to Yemen. There were several reasons for her decision.

He had been a dead weight. More interested in his career as a television journalist than in her and he was trying to get back with her, now he found out she might be related to a celebrity. Or even one herself, when they managed to rescue Matt. No way would she take Nick back again.

When Conor met her at Sana'a Airport, he was wearing a sand-colored suit which definitely made the most of his muscles. It was the kind of suit that begged a woman to investigate what lay underneath the thin material. She got the feeling his body would be like one of the male nudes photographed by Testino, which she framed and hung on the wall in the hall of her London flat. It always did her good to come home after a trying day and look at the guy's broad-shouldered torso, his great six pack and narrow tapering hips, where the photo cut off leaving the rest to the imagination.

She shivered with excitement, thinking how the man she was going to spend the next few weeks with would look under that suit, and a brief, tantalizing throb ran through her just thinking about it. She had been convinced when they met for the very first time he was not a man, who sat at a desk all day. At that initial meeting, they shook hands only briefly, but his hand, clasped in hers, felt warm and firm, which was a good sign. If there was anything Lucy hated, it was a cold, fishy palm. Conor's handshake inspired confidence and she needed as much of that as she could get, given how vulnerable she was feeling.

She read up on him on the journey to Sana. A Cambridge graduate, now a civil servant—probably fast-track—who was an expert on

Yemeni tribes. In her imagination he'd been earnest and bespectacled, the epitome of the cool Englishman. How wrong she had been. Confronting such a miracle of unconventionality at the airport had been quite an experience and continued to be so, she thought.

Lucy looked down once more. Here and there she could see what seemed to be a village clinging to a crag, with thin lines of white tracks climbing crazily upwards. Goat tracks.

'Poor sods,' Conor said suddenly. She raised her eyebrows. His eyes were dark and brooding. She couldn't imagine what he was thinking, but this was a side of him she hadn't seen so far. 'I mean on the ground,' he indicated. 'Their lives must be bloody awful.' He was looking down.

'Perhaps they don't mind?' she replied. Afterwards, she could have bitten off her tongue, because she perceived the tiniest glimmer of hostility in his glance, which told her he didn't think much of the remark and, she had to admit, the question had been remarkably smug.

'I can assure you they do, Miss Page,' he replied, pulling his brows together into a frown and staring her straight in the eyes. 'The landscape might look dramatic. Even beautiful to you but, down there, they live in houses, where the walls are lined with cow dung and

13

sand and it's a six mile walk to the local well for water. If there is one.'

Lucy stiffened. He didn't have to be so patronizing, even if she did deserve it. Once again, she felt that little throb inside. She didn't want him to think she was shallow, but she had to let him know she wasn't naïve about the place and the people.

'I think you're forgetting something, Mr Kendall,' she returned levelly. 'I'm not a complete novice. Nor entirely ignorant of what goes on down there.' She would have liked to add that she cut her teeth on its legends, but she wasn't going to.

'I'm relieved to hear it. It'll make my job easier,' he said curtly, turning back to his conversation with the pilot.

He felt the atmosphere as he concentrated. Lucy had the fighting spirit all right. He grinned to himself. At least, it would make his dangerous mission more interesting. He was glad she could stand up to him. It was a good sign, although he was a bit sorry he'd bitten. He knew he wasn't in the best of moods. Most of all because they were running behind schedule. Which meant that, if he did not meet Khalid on time, the deal could be off.

He didn't know why but, for some reason, the pilot had been held up. When he finally arrived, he could see the guy was wet behind the ears. While he went over the pre-flight checks, Conor had been concentrating on

14

getting Lucy Page's luggage stowed safely. It was all unnecessary stress and, in his profession, he couldn't afford to be stressed.

He had a deadline to meet, but it seemed the wind had other ideas and it was bringing the sand along with it. At least the Yemeni Army possessed choppers suited to desert terrain.

He had seen the damage sand in the air intakes could do and he wanted nothing to go wrong, especially with this woman on board. He had managed to get over the feeling he was a jinx to women, but it had taken a very long time. He forced the memory of Leila away. It still hurt.

He could feel his present companion's eyes strafing his back. He realized he had offended her and he had not been entirely fair. He had done his homework on Lucy Page's background. It had been absolutely necessary, given the mission.

He'd read her impressive biography. School of Oriental and African Studies, London University. Arabic, first class. Doctorate three years later.

But clever or cultured was rarely any defense when a loaded pistol was being pointed at your head. Hopefully, she would not follow in her illustrious father's footsteps.

Conor considered the reputation of the famous Professor Page, whose name was still well known in cultured circles in the Yemen.

15

The archaeologist was held a Byronic figure, who had spent a great deal of his life conducting expeditions under the auspices of the University of Aden. That was when the British controlled South Yemen.

But, after the political turmoil of the recent past, it was becoming much harder to go treasure hunting, a fact, which Matt Page discovered to his cost.

The late professor was rumored to have preferred the thrill of working in the wild places of the Yemen to a peaceable academic career in England, but he paid dearly for the doubtful privilege.

After thirty years of doing what he loved most, he contracted a serious infection, which claimed his life. He died ignominiously in a hut outside the village of Mokata. The only friend at his deathbed had been his Arab servant, who remained faithful to him for years.

Conor shook his head imperceptibly. The professor sacrificed home and family for what? The treasures of the Yemen?

First the father, then the son. Now it seemed the daughter was on the case. What a family.

And it was up to him not to let the same thing happen to her. He sniffed. The sand still got to him.

His greatest desire was to go on living for as long as he could. Life was for enjoying while it lasted. And he hadn't had much chance for enjoyment lately. He stared morosely down at the landscape as the chopper cruised at one hundred and fifty miles per hour. Then he glanced quickly at Lucy, which cheered him up.

Lucy blazed inside. At herself and him . . . She knew she'd been asking for it, but she hated sarcasm. Besides, his eyes twinkled annoyingly when he'd rebuked her. As if it was a game and he was making fun of her. How dare he? He thought she didn't know anything and she couldn't look after herself.

She stared out of the chopper, taking deep breaths. What could she expect from a man, who was making it very clear he thought she wasn't up to such a dangerous enterprise?

She recalled one episode in particular which occurred during the forty-eight hours after he delivered her at the British Consulate for her briefing, then taken her on to her hotel.

In the early evening, he telephoned her room and asked her to meet him in the foyer. Lucy had just come out of the shower and was feeling extremely tired. Strung-up by heat and excitement, she was also rather irritable and had been expecting to fall into bed, but her bad mood diminished at the thought of being introduced to Sana'a by him. Wrong again.

She kept him waiting, deciding what was the best thing to wear. When she emerged from her hotel's foyer in smart evening wear, satisfied that she looked good, she realized her mistake straightaway. She'd dressed up and Conor was attired on the downside of casual in a camouflage flak jacket open to the waist and matching khaki chinos. She couldn't help looking at the revelatory expanse of smooth tanned skin and luxuriant chest hair.

She also knew he'd noticed those surreptitious glances of hers. He grinned back annoyingly, so she pulled down her fashionable shades from where they were perched high on her hair and looked to her heart's content. Unfortunately, the taxi ride they took was short and uneventful, and, surprise, surprise, soon they were back at the Consulate and emerging from the lift at basement level.

A strange look appeared in his dark eyes as they stood together in that windowless cavern below ground. Lucy took off her glasses because it was so dark she couldn't see a thing. She looked round.

Locked grey steel cupboards lined the stark, white walls. Then he was opening a wooden crate, which was standing on a table, A moment later, he brought out a bullet-proof vest which he handed over for her to try.

'What's this, then?' she'd grimaced, staring at the bulky-looking waistcoat.

'A bullet-proof vest. It's for your own safety.' His whimsical expression annoyed her. He wrongly assumed her question had been straightforward.

'I know what it is, Conor, but . . . are we expecting to be shot?' It had been meant as a joke, but it fell flat and she was angry, because their mission to release Matt was the most important thing in the world, but that was Lucy's way, making light of things that really mattered.

'We may be shot at.' The considered remark was delivered without any change of expression or tone. She'd shivered. What was she afraid of? Of fielding a bullet from some madman's gun? Of finding Matt in a terrible state? Even worse, of not finding him.

'Well, as long as they aim low,' she'd quipped, feeling somewhat less than brave inside. She was angry with herself for feeling so apprehensive.

'They probably will,' he'd replied and, suddenly, he'd been looking at her body with as much interest as she'd stared at his. She'd shaken off the sudden surge of attraction she felt for him, which was running like warm treacle through her lowest parts. To cover both her fears and confusion, she'd quipped, 'What about my head?'

'You keep it down,' he'd retorted, turning unsympathetic again. It was then she realized his moods were like pieces of quicksilver. She squashed the sudden disappointment that came from his rebuff.

She told herself firmly it was not comfort

19

she wanted from him. Only action, and the promise to get Matt and herself back safe to civilization, but that was in the future. This was the here and now.

Lucy dragged herself into the present. Conor told her they would be meeting their guide at the dropping off place designated in the foothills of the high massif. After that they would be continuing the journey by Land Rover.

Where they were driving to, she didn't know, although she gleaned it was to some remote village where the terrorists were holed up. If so much had not depended upon it, it would have been a real adventure.

She told herself she had no right to feel excited. It was more sensible to be apprehensive. Her father thrived on 'adventure' and look what happened to him. She often thought about her father and the isolated place where he'd died. She could only pray it wasn't going to happen to her.

The Yemen possessed a troubled history but since the merger of the two states of Yemen and South Yemen in 1990, the military purported to be united against terrorist factions and Conor had said there were government forces to call on, if they were needed . . .

He came out of his reverie. He swung round again, his eyebrows lifting in that irritating way. 'Something on your mind? Can I help?'

20

he asked. He was trying to help, but he knew, by the look on her face, she thought he was being sarcastic.

'I was thinking about Khalid,' she said, fishing. 'I suppose that, as our guide, he has a fund of local knowledge at his fingertips.'

'Ah, Khalid,' he said, leaning back easily. 'He's a very interesting fellow.' He was, because, as Conor knew only too well, Khalid was their only hope of getting close to Abdul. The kidnapper had a serious price on his head, but, if negotiations went well and the price was right, there was a possibility Abdul might be persuaded to release his hostage. However, the negotiations could easily fail, since Abdul was both an extremely unstable and highly dangerous man. They had tangled before, although Conor intended to keep that information under his belt for the time being.

'Why? What's he like?'

Her face was somber. Clearly, Lucy needed to believe he was a genius at his job. He watched as she looked away and down as the helicopter whirled on, listening to the comforting, steady thump of its engines. Noting the set line of her lips, he found himself thinking she would be extremely pretty if only she smiled more.

'I'd say . . .' he considered, '. . . I'd say Khalid is a mixture of intellectual and assassin.' That did the trick. She was staring at him.

'You're joking.'

'I'm not.'

Surprise lit up her face. 'Who is he? Why do we want him as a guide? Have you worked with him before?'

He realized he'd alarmed her by his choice of the word 'assassin'.

'Steady on. One thing at a time.'

Lucy sighed inwardly. The man had the unfortunate knack of being able to startle and annoy her at the same time and she didn't like not being in control.

'He's very well-educated. England, of course, like a lot of well-to-do Yemeni. Soldiering. If you could call it that. He's also lectured in Politics at the University of Aden.'

He glanced at her face. Careful, he warned. Get off that tack. You're probably reminding her of her father. We want her staying tough.

He went on: 'In fact, Khalid's in your league. A religious expert and philosopher as well.'

'I'm a linguist,' snapped Lucy. 'What about the "assassin" bit?'

'I was getting on to that,' he stressed, wishing she was more patient. He was trying to be nice, although he clearly needn't have bothered but, at least, he admitted to himself, it was a break from the boredom of the long flight having someone sparky to talk to. The pilot was a bone head.

'Khalid is an expert on Arabian matters,' he

continued. 'A former governor of the post-independence states, which were swallowed up in the unification of . . .'

'Okay,' said Lucy, 'I know the history. What about him? Why is he being used as a guide for us?'

He frowned. She was beginning to seriously annoy him.

'The place we're heading for—where we think your brother's being held—is terrain Khalid knows well. Better than anyone, in fact. Frankly, we have been lucky to get hold of him.'

Conor knew there could have been no one else for this particular job, but it had been touch and go whether the Arab would agree to the conditions. How Khalid was persuaded to volunteer his services had been nothing to do with him, but he knew things were never done for nothing in his business.

The two men had worked together before, but Conor had no intention of giving Lucy Page that sort of information.

But, when he and Khalid met, which was rare nowadays, neither of them ever mentioned their painful past. He smiled ruefully. Lucy made a face.

'What's funny?' she asked. 'You still haven't explained the assassin part.'

He shrugged. 'I'm not always serious.'

'You could have fooled me,' she snapped.

He struggled. 'There's bound to be an

23

element of assassination in tribal struggles. I've no hard evidence, of course. However, when he was young, Khalid was the powerful leader of a warlike tribe.' He considered that would do as a fair remark about the Arab's character.

'How old is he?' Lucy asked, cooling off.

'Early fifties?'

She shook her head and caught his gaze, not realizing she was looking at him from under her long lashes. 'Sorry, I'm a bit wound up,' she confessed, smiling in response. He was evidently trying to make amends. Perhaps he wasn't quite so bad? And he had the most devastating smile. It transformed his face.

'That's okay,' he replied. 'We all are.'

*   *   *

Soon, he was looking keenly at his maps, but something else was on his mind too, which was unprofessional. Lucy's smile stirred up something inside himself, which he had almost forgotten and still wanted to forget. As much as Khalid. Given the awful circumstances.

He shook off the thought, jerking himself back to the present. He had been right. Her lips were great and that look from under her eyelashes even better. He wasn't a mind reader. Was Lucy Page winding him up?

They flew on, the helicopter's nose pointed in the direction of the mountains, which were

24

increasing in size every minute.

'How far now?' asked Lucy. His words stung her hard but, by then, she had seen sense and swallowed back the animosity she felt for his lack of sensitivity.

He looked at his watch. 'An hour or so.' She leaned back, mentally going over the kit she brought with her. It had all been waiting for her, ready and prepared in another room in the depth of the Consulate's basement. He insisted going through it fastidiously.

'Wool sweater, long underwear, wool stocking cap for the cold evenings and nights . . .' In spite of the air conditioning, Lucy had been sweating in very light cotton at the time. The thought of wearing any of that was horrific.

'Goggles, scarves . . . for your mouth and nose when the sand is swirling . . . T shirts to wear under your uniform . . . they soak up the sweat.'

'Uniform?'

'A bit like camouflage . . . but not quite. It will help you fade into the landscape.' She didn't query it. Best not to. He must know what he was doing. She only hoped the tribesmen wouldn't take her for a soldier.

'Water supply . . .' he looked at her obliquely. '. . . At temperatures above 38 degrees you have to drink a litre of water per hour. I'll be carrying what we'll need until we make contact with Khalid.'

Afterwards, she watched as he checked that a pistol was unloaded before handing it to her. She stared at it weakly. 'It's a Glock,' he said helpfully.

'Thanks. Nice to be prepared.'

And then those dark eyes of his strafed her face as he handed her the ammunition.

'Hopefully, there'll be no need to use it. Have you ever loaded one of these?' He began to show her how to do so. 'Or fired one?' She could see by his face he was expecting her to say no.

'It may come as a surprise to you,' she said, 'But, actually, I have.' He lifted his eyebrows as he placed the weapon carefully down. 'My school took part in Bisley.'

'Fantastic.' She could have sworn the corners of his mouth were fighting not to smile, but it was true. She had been small arms champion at her boarding school, but she had never thought her talent as a shot might prove to be useful.

Then all the other equipment was added. Her back pack looked very bulky, and when he helped her try it on, she found it incredibly heavy.

She glanced at the humped green mountain, that must have been his, and gritted her teeth, trying not to show her dismay.

One good thing, Lucy had made use of the last few months, before she flew to the Yemen, working out and jogging every morning and evening.

She had been priming herself, psyching herself up to manage the kind of terrain she knew she would have to face if she ever got the chance to look for Matt. Now, she intended to cope.

Hopefully, she could surprise Conor again and show him she was no wimp, but the pack wasn't light.

When he helped her off with it, he added, 'I've left a few things out in case it was too heavy. Don't worry about it, I'm well prepared.'

'I'm sure you are,' she said with a hint of sarcasm.

'And, if it gets too heavy, I can always help.'

'That's very good of you.' Their conversation continued to be stilted.

That morning, she had put on the protective vest. Its wadding was stiflingly warm, but she hadn't questioned his orders as to why she should wear the bullet-proof vest on a helicopter ride.

It was compressing her breasts uncomfortably. She remembered reading in a tabloid newspaper about some London policewoman complaining to her superiors about just that. Lucy never thought she would be in the same position.

She wriggled about to get comfortable and was rewarded by a keen glance from him. It was all right for him. He had only his pecs to worry about.

Instinct told her he knew what was the matter. It was the way his eyes drifted above her waist and sized up what was happening under her green camouflage jacket.

Perhaps she could slip off the vest once they landed. Then she realized how impractical that would be. She'd rather be uncomfortably hot than the target of a bullet from one of Abdul's men. Was it really that bad down there?

Suddenly, she looked forward, realizing both Conor and the young pilot were leaning forward intently, peering at the dials. Lucy's instincts must have been finely tuned, because a tiny tickle of uneasiness made her sit up and take notice.

Something was wrong.

'Christ! The fuel monitor must have been giving a false reading.'

'It was all right on the checks.'

'Well, it isn't now. The pressure's dropping,' snarled Conor. 'How far are we from the drop off point now?'

'Fifteen minutes. We're going to have to go down.'

Lucy ignored the two-way radio communications in Arabic, which came in at regular intervals. She couldn't make head nor tail of them. Now she was listening to everything very carefully.

'The wind's affecting the blades,' shouted

28

the pilot. 'We have to drop her.'

'Well, vary the pitch angle,' ordered Conor. Briefly, Lucy wondered why he was not flying the helicopter.

Maybe he should have been, because he seemed to know a lot more about it than the young Yemeni, who was acting nervously, his left hand moving a lever gingerly up and down. 'She's not responding,' he shouted.

Momentarily, Lucy wondered where the man had been trained. She hoped that his instructors knew what they were doing.

'Steady now,' warned Conor, clamping his hand over the other's. She didn't like the look on her companion's face.

'Is something the matter?' She had to speak.

'Shush,' snarled Conor, as the chopper veered jerkily, then righted itself again.

Lucy subsided, angrily. She looked down. The ground seemed a hell of a long way. This was all she needed. It wasn't a nice feeling.

'Give her some throttle.' The pilot complied. Whether he didn't know what he was doing, or he didn't care about someone telling him what to do, was academic now. They were evidently in some kind of trouble. 'Altitude?' The pilot was reading off the figures.

'Shit.' They sat motionless.

'What's happening?' She heard her voice come out like a squeak. Nothing like normal.

Conor shook his head at her. He looked at

the pilot. 'Start looking for a place.'

The pilot was leaning and looking outside. 'Let base know what's happening,' said Conor. Lucy strained her ears as the pilot spoke urgently over the radio in rapid Arabic. Gone were the ordered, staccato tones. He was shouting.

Her command of the language was very good, but she could only make out a bit, given the noise the helicopter was churning out now and the bad reception.

'Is it something to do with the fuel?' she screamed. There was no way she was going to sit there like a dummy.

'Yes.' That was the only explanation he offered. The pilot turned to Conor.

'They have our position. Allah be praised.'

'You hope. Now, try to get her down on the plateau.' He swung round to Lucy. 'Well, you know the score. I'm sorry, Miss Page, but we're going to have to crash land. He's trying for the wadi.' She bit her lips. 'Believe me, it will be better than the side of the mountain. It all depends on the wind, but it won't be pretty.'

'Will it explode?' It was all she could think of.

'No,' he said. She swallowed. Then a faint smile followed. 'Don't worry, we won't be that unlucky.'

'What's gone wrong?' The chopper's erratic behavior was terrifying.

'Let's keep the post mortem for later, shall

we.' She didn't like his sense of humor one little bit.

Seconds after, he was going through the crash landing proceedings with her. Steadily. Carefully. As if he had all the time in the world. Coolly, as though he was explaining to a child about to take a boat ride on a pool in the park.

Meanwhile bchind her, the tail rotor was swinging wildly effecting the change in the blades' direction and they were swinging down and down. Circling cyclically.

'Clear?' he questioned tersely. She nodded. 'You might get a few bruises.'

'If I'm lucky,' she quipped. He was glad she hadn't started screaming.

He brcathed in to calm himself, deciding it must have been sabotage. At least, the bastard hadn't cut the fuel pipe. Hc had seen the fireballs, which exploding helicopters made, too many times but, by the way the dials had been behaving, he suspected someone had severely damaged the hydraulics.

He glanced at the girl's white face, sorry that it seemed as though his worst fears were being realized.

Yes. Leave the post mortem until later. As long as it isn't ours, he told himself grimly.

As the young pilot battled with the retractable landing gcar, Conor tried to convince himself Abdul was so keen on getting hold of the arms which were part of the conditions for the release of Matt Page, that he wouldn't have ordered one of his henchmen to blow them out of the sky.

With that, Conor half-crouched into the position he'd explained to Lucy and stretched out his hand backwards to the girl. 'Here, hold on,' he said, 'and pray.'

Lucy closed her eyes in trepidation, but they opened wide with surprise as he took her cold, small hand in his warm one.

Somehow, that little human gesture was something she could not have done without. Next moment, the helicopter plunged nose down towards the mountain plateau's broken dissected terrain.

And, all the time, the Arab pilot wrestled with the controls, calling frantically on a beneficent Allah to grant them a favorable place to crash.

Chapter Two

Lucy's chest felt crushed and flattened by that crazy plummeting through space as the chopper fell one thousand feet out of the sky.

Her ears were a bubble of searing and hissing noise as she held on to the last vestige of reality. Conor's strong fingers linked with hers.

Then their clasp tore apart on impact with the ground and Lucy was all alone. Surrounded by silence.

A second later, a deep thumping started in her ear drums, which she recognized as her frantic heart.

She breathed in and swallowed to ease her dry mouth, then opened her eyes to masses of twisted metal. She was still alive. She couldn't believe it. She'd survived the crash landing.

Then mad panic replaced that eerie calm. As she struggled to move, she felt a sudden, sharp pain stabbing her. When she looked down, she almost fainted. A long piece of metal appeared to be sticking out of her side. 'Oh, my God.' She began to scream. She was trapped.

Her voice sounded like it didn't belong to her. The twisted metal, which had been the roof, whirled around her in that terrible moment of panic.

Then strong hands grabbed her shoulders. 'Stop it. Snap out of it.' His urgent words seemed totally brutal. She shook with shock and fright, tears running down her cheeks. 'Are you hurt?'

'Conor, Conor. Look, look!' she screamed. She could feel his warm breath comforting her cheek as he leaned right over her, his arms holding her body tightly.

She squinted down, her lips twisted with pain and fear. He was about to touch the piece of metal. 'No, no, don't, please.' He stopped, his eyes were willing her to calm down.

'I have to move it, Lucy. We have to get out. Away from the chopper.'

'No, no!' she shouted.

'Calm down,' he ordered. 'Pull yourself together. You're okay if you're talking.'

'But . . .' She stared at the side of his face as his probing eyes concentrated on the metal again. His cheek was cut, badly swollen. She closed her eyes, her mind listening to him in a daze.

'Now do what I tell you. Right.' He soothed. 'Move your legs.' She could. 'Now your arms. Wiggle them,' he commanded, his voice shaky with tension. She obeyed. He took hold of the metal.

'Okay.' She threw back her head so she couldn't see what he was doing. 'Does this hurt?' She could feel nothing. She shook her head. She dare not look, but she knew he was

34

grabbing the rod. 'Good. Now, lean right back.'

'What are you going to do?'

'What I have to,' he said. 'Listen. You haven't been impaled. You have been saved by the vest. Kevlar is very flexible material. It doesn't let metal through.' He added. 'You're only trapped in the seat. I'm getting you out.'

He was talking to her like a child while she was fighting not to be sick. 'There.' He was pulling very hard with both hands, his muscles straining.

'Got it.' There was a sickening scraping. He let out a deep sigh from the exertion. 'Now can you move?' She was frightened to. 'Can you move, Lucy?' he repeated urgently. She tried.

'Yes.'

He straightened. His face was pale. 'Good. You were only pinned to the seat. Come on.' Next moment he caught her by the shoulders and was pulling her up.

'Ouch,' she protested weakly. Her side hurt like hell. 'Wait a moment.' She grabbed her holdall, which had been jammed beside her in the seat.

'Leave it,' he commanded, but she disobeyed him, hanging on to it, trying to concentrate on anything but the pain.

'Now!' He dragged her, like some pathetic doll, over the mangled remains of the cockpit, which hissed ominously. Then they were

35

running and, next moment, Lucy collapsed on the stony earth.

He was on one knee beside her.

'Are you okay?'

'I don't know.' She was trying to get herself together. 'I feel faint.' Her face was very pale. He pushed her head down.

'Keep your head between your knees and stay like that,' he barked. 'I have to go back in.'

'What?' she shouted, lifting her eyes to look. His tall figure was already disappearing inside the wreckage. For one second, panic overcame her again. What if he didn't get out? She'd be left all on her own.

She looked round, her head clearing. The chopper had come down in a flat arid area, a kind of canyon, but very broad and wide. A desert landscape of scrub and sand, which stretched right up to the steep walls of the nearest mountain.

She shivered at how near they must have been to hitting it. Far away in the distance, she could see the shapes of the massif.

Suddenly, it reminded her of her first glimpse of the Alps. She had been about ten and on holiday with Matt and her parents. It had been sunset like it was now. 'Look at the peaks,' Matt had shouted.

'Where? I can't see them,' she'd retorted, staring in front of her.

'Not down there, silly. Look up. Up in the sky.' And their tops had been floating in a sea of golden cloud, the snow looking like strawberry ice cream.

Everything had been beautiful when they were all together as a family. She had been so happy, but these mountains were looming, unfriendly and black, as the sun went down. Tears started in Lucy's eyes. For God's sake, you are not going to cry, she told herself. It's the shock that's making you behave like an idiot.

Then sense and relief took over. Conor was staggering out of the wreckage. Slung over his shoulders was the pilot.

Ignoring her own pain, Lucy struggled to her feet and stumbled to meet them. 'I'll help.'

'You can't. Not now.' He was breathing heavily and sweat was running down his face. 'Look after yourself first.' She was limping along beside him like a small dog. Then he stopped and let the man slide down his back.

Lucy supported the pilot as he crumpled on to the ground. A second later, Conor was kneeling beside him.

'What do we do?' asked Lucy. She had never felt more useless as she joined him. The pilot's face was pale and there was blood trickling from both corners of his mouth. He lay there, white and completely still. Instinctively, Lucy knew he was seriously hurt. 'Is he unconscious?'

He shook his head in answer to her question. He was checking to see if the pilot was still breathing. Then, after putting an ear to his chest and feeling the young man's wrist again, he looked up at Lucy and shook his head.

She sat back on her heels, closing her eyes momentarily, praying he was wrong. Why couldn't Conor save him, like he'd saved her? The man seemed practically superhuman even though he had been hurt himself. She noticed a weal on his cheek, which was oozing dark blood.

'You're bleeding,' she said calmly, consciously erasing any tremble from her voice. Those few moments of sheer panic were over. She was determined to be self-possessed, but if she had been her usual self, she would have been very angry at the way she behaved under pressure.

'Mine's only a scratch. Tetanus will take care of it, but . . .' He looked down. 'I don't think there's much I can do for him.'

'But he's so young,' she said, her face drained of blood. She was thinking about the metal strut, which she'd imagined sticking out of her side. Thank God for the bullet-proof vest, and for doing as she was told. Conor stood up.

'There must be something you can do,' cried Lucy. She watched dumbly as he leaned over and checked the pulse again in the young Arab's neck.

He shook his head. 'There's nothing. I'm

afraid he's had it.'

'It's horrible.' Her face crumpled.

'Massive internal bleeding I expect,' he explained, noting her pale face. 'We've been very lucky.' He could see how upset she was. He had seen several men die, and he never got used to it, but he tried not to show concern in his expression. It was an unwritten rule in his profession. He was in charge and he had to keep up morale. He felt mentioning the fact they had been lucky might do her some good, but it didn't seem to work. She started to cry. He put a hand on her shoulder and he could feel the sobs shaking her frame.

'What are we going to do?' she asked, looking up at him with frightened eyes.

He considered his answer carefully, although there was only one solution. He must bury him, so they could get on their way. Although Lucy needed to know what was happening, Conor also realized an insensitive answer would do more harm than good. 'I'll tell you in a minute,' he stalled. 'You stay here with him, while I go back to the chopper and get some stuff out?'

'You're not going in there again. Please?' she begged.

'We need our kit.'

'But is it safe? It might blow up.' She was still afraid of the crashed helicopter exploding. Lucy couldn't bear the thought of him leaving her, sitting uselessly by the dead pilot. She was afraid something else terrible might happen and she would be left all on her own.

'If it was going to explode, it would have by now,' he reassured. 'Try not to worry. I won't be in there long.'

Those moments of waiting were some of the worst Lucy ever experienced. She felt her heart in her ears again as her mind and soul begged him to re-appear. All the time he was gone, she did her best not to look at the pilot's body, but she felt a need to do something, so she recited some Arabic prayers, which seemed the right thing in the circumstances.

Then, suddenly, her spirits lifted as she saw Conor hurrying back, hunched under the weight of his kit bag. She swallowed as she realized he was carrying a short spade as well. He dropped it a few meters away and slipped off his pack.

'We'll have to share. Yours has had it. Crushed,' he said, arching his back. 'Whew.' She was still looking at the spade. He followed her eyes. 'The best thing for you to do now is go over where you were before. You should try to rest after the shock.'

'You're going to bury him,' she stated dully.

'I have to. Anyway, you know that's what would have happened straightaway if he died at home.'

She nodded. Islamic law decreed a swift interment. 'I don't know how you can,' she said softly.

40

He hoped she wasn't going to be sick. She looked distraught and pale. 'Come on,' he said. 'Just keep on thinking how lucky we have been to get off with a few bruises. I'm sorry about the poor chap too, but we still have a job to do. To rescue your brother, and the quicker we get on with it, the better.'

After she limped thirty meters or so away, Conor dragged the body behind the crashed helicopter. The job took him ages.

After he'd finished burying the body, he shook off the thought of what he had just done. He had to keep going, keep up his spirit and hers but, when he returned, he was sweating heavily. There were dark circles under his eyes and his face was strained. 'Pity that old crate wasn't fitted with G.P.S.' he replied, indicating the chopper. He fielded Lucy's puzzled look. 'Global Positioning System. As you go down, your position can be pin-pointed and rescuers are with you in less than an hour. Unfortunately, this chopper was an old one and wasn't fitted up with it.'

'What will happen now?'

'It'll have to be search and rescue. Hopefully, they got our signal. No chance of trying again. The communications are smashed and I have no two-way radio with me.' He cursed himself. They were too bulky to carry on a mission like this. He continued the explanation: 'If they didn't, they'll be out looking when the chopper doesn't return on

41

time.'

She listened to his explanations, knowing that in this dry bone of a place, she was a babe-in-arms compared with Conor. Silent questions about the man crowded Lucy's head. When she'd first met him, she suspected he was not desk bound. Now she was sure her suspicions were correct and she was glad she'd been right, because the thought of being stranded out here with some office worker would have frightened her to death.

She acknowledged his superiority, but discomfort was gnawing. She wanted him to believe she was up to this trek, given his apparently scathing opinion as to her stamina. What the hell did he think about her now, after her behavior under pressure?

But he didn't seem to notice how she was feeling. Lucy didn't know what to say, so she kept quiet. It was the first time she had ever seen a dead body, never mind one buried like that. Meanwhile, he was checking and re-checking their supplies. He took out two containers and began to measure the water from one into the other. He turned to Lucy. 'There were supplies in the helicopter, but they were smashed in the impact.'

He added, 'There's enough water for both of us. It should last about five hours. They're bound to be here by then. We have to make it last.' Then he started counting out some small packages.

42

'What are those?' asked Lucy.

'Compo rations. Luckily we don't have to mix them with water like we used to. They're a bit like biscuits now. Anyway, you and I need to talk. To get things into proportion.'

He breathed in deeply. 'We have to forget what's just happened. We've come out of it in one piece and we have to survive until we meet Khalid. If for some reason he doesn't keep the rendezvous, we'll stay around there until we're picked up.'

Lucy was angry with herself that he had to spell it out to her. He thought she was a complete wreck.

'I'm not a child,' she retorted. Attack has always been Lucy's way of defending herself, even in tomboyish fights with Matt but, inside, a voice was telling her that, out here, she was completely naïve, compared with him and, in spite of all she had been through that day, she couldn't help resenting the fact.

'Then stop behaving like one,' he answered.

'But, surely, it would be better to stay at the crash site. Where they are sure to find us.' She realized her obstinate remark showed she was questioning his judgment again. Conor looked in no mood to argue. She knew it was sensible to do what he told her, or they would be in serious trouble, but she was annoyed by his evident lack of faith in her.

'No, I don't. I agree it's against SOP.' She didn't understand, then he explained.

43

'Standard Operation Procedure leaving here, but we have a deadline to meet Khalid. It's going to take some time for search and rescue to get here. By then, we might have lost the chance to get to Abdul. Khalid knows the score. We have to make the rendezvous. You need to trust me on this.'

'I do but . . .' She really wanted to, but was used to expressing her own opinion on everything.

'There are no buts. HQ . . .' She lifted her eyebrows. 'Government Forces and my bosses know where we're meeting him. If anything goes wrong and he isn't there, they'll pick us up.' He had convinced her, but Lucy felt he was still treating her as if she was a child but, anyway, knowing she had other strengths, she forced herself to listen patiently as he explained.

'But, until we do, we shan't know about Abdul. Whether Khalid's been able to fix it. Or what we have to do. Whether to go straight to our base in the mountains, or straight on to Abdul's camp. So we have to be there. Do you understand? If we have a chance of getting your brother back, we have to meet Khalid.' He breathed in deeply.

'There is another option. You could stay here. I'd leave you water and food. It would be best.' Her eyes almost flashed sparks when she was angry.

'And that's what you want, isn't it? That's

what you have wanted from the start. You have never wanted me on this mission.'

'Don't get hysterical,' he said. 'Save your breath.'

'I'm not hysterical,' cried Lucy, wiping the sweat from her brow. 'I haven't waited all these months to be left sitting pretty by a crashed helicopter. If you're going, I am. Oh . . .' The pain shot through her side.

'What's up?'

'Just . . . bruises.' The word was sharp.

Touché, Lucy, he thought. 'Let's have a look.' Suddenly, he was afraid she had been injured internally and he cursed himself he hadn't checked. 'Take it off.' She stared at him. 'The vest. Take it off. Here let me help.'

She didn't remonstrate as he undid it, but she groaned as he pulled the Velcro apart. 'Now your jacket and your shirt.'

'I . . .' She wasn't wearing a bra. She'd felt too congested under the bullet-proof vest and the camouflage.

'It doesn't matter. I need to check. Just in case.' The clouds over the mountains looked like they'd been soaked with black ink. Soon it would be dark as the desert night fell swiftly.

He helped her off with her top. She moved carefully around, folding her arms over her naked breasts as his careful fingers moved over her back and sides. She was badly bruised where the strut had pinned her.

45

'Sorry,' he murmured as she winced at his touch. 'I'm no doctor but I'm pretty sure you've hurt your ribs.' His exploring fingers were counting them mentally, but he was thinking of the words from Bab al-Nikah:

Admonish your wives with kindness, because women were created from a crooked bone of the side. Therefore if you wish to straighten it, you will break it, and if you let it alone, it will always be crooked.

She put her head down. 'Does it hurt when you breathe in?' he asked softly.

'Not much,' she muttered. All she could think of then was he was going to ask her to turn round.

'Well, you haven't bust one,' he said. 'Would you turn round, please?'

'But . . .' she began.

He sat back on his heels. 'I'm sorry, Miss Page, but this is no time for false modesty.' She breathed in. He was right and he was the only help around. 'I need to check if your stomach's okay.'

'My stomach?' she murmured.

'Yes. I'll be as quick as I can.' Lucy complied, letting her hands fall to her sides. She turned towards him, closing her eyes at the same time.

He attempted to detach himself from the task. He needed to make sure she wasn't bleeding internally. To look for any sign of swelling in the soft tissue of the diaphragm.

46

God, but she was beautiful. He couldn't help looking at her breasts.

They were small and firm. Suddenly, he realized she wasn't wearing a bra. He put the idea out of his mind as his fingers felt the soft skin under her rib cage. He swore at himself under his breath. He looked into her strained, white face and forced himself to calm down.

He had punished his body over these last few years since he lost Leila. He had promised himself no woman would ever get to him again. Emotion was dangerous. He must not let it get to him. He had been afraid of something like this happening, and now, he was saddled with a female, who would be nothing but a drag on him in desert terrain.

The thought of his escape with Leila briefly crossed his mind, but Lucy Page was no Arab.

He wished he could be different, but they needed to survive. There was no way the English girl could walk more than five kilometers a night, and they couldn't walk in the day. Hopefully, they wouldn't have to if Khalid was where he should be.

He'd had women since Leila, used them, enjoyed sex on the simplest level.

Her nipples stood out, pink and delectable. He squashed the ridiculous thought she was enjoying this too. She couldn't stand him, he knew that and no wonder. He was becoming a brute these days.

47

But he was all stirred up inside. He sat back. She opened her eyes. His voice was level. 'You're okay, there's no swelling. You can thank the Kevlar for saving your life. That metal strut must have given you a hell of a bang but, luckily, you were well protected.'

'Thank you,' she murmured. He handed her top over and looked away as she put it on. His emotions were fighting with his professional sense.

'Now where was I?' he asked.

'You were telling me why we had to leave.' Lucy had recovered too. Feeling his gentle hands probing her body was the most pleasurable thing she'd experienced for a very long time.

She hated herself for even thinking it. You've just survived a plane crash and seen a man die. You're out here all alone in the desert with an arrogant bastard like him and you're imagining having sex with him. Get a life, please, she told herself.

'Yes. We've a deadline, which we have to make if we want to get your brother out. We can only travel at night and we've wasted enough time already.'

He was looking in the kit bag. Now the sun had disappeared, it was getting cold. Lucy shivered. 'Here,' he added, 'put on this shirt and my sweater. They'll be too big, but they'll have to do.'

'What about you?'

'I've another somewhere. Anyway, I'm used to it. More or less.' He kept on saying stupid things about what she might have to face, telling her about wild animals and things like that. He didn't take his eyes off her as she dressed. The T shirt swamped her. 'Suits you,' he said. 'Let's hope we don't hit a storm.'

'Why?'

'We've only one pair of goggles left and one scarf.'

'Oh,' was all she could manage, realizing what predicament faced them.

'Now. Have a drink. It's rationed.' She looked doubtful.

'I can manage at the moment.'

'No, you can't. You think you can but you need to drink some water at least once an hour in the day time, but not so much at night.' He looked up. 'Hopefully, there'll be a moon tonight. Moonlight over here makes the terrain crystal clear.

'There's nothing like a desert moon,' he added quietly. Lucy looked at him sharply. It was the way he said it. 'The wind dies down in the night. All this haze that has been swamping us, the glare of the afternoon, it'll all disappear. You can see and hear for miles if anyone's around.'

'You make it sound beautiful,' she replied doubtfully, struggling to her feet.

'It is, but it's not like a night in England,' he said, picking up his kit bag. She helped him.

49

He looked at her, surprised.

'Thank you. Come on. If they haven't found us by dawn, I'll be surprised. They'll know we've gone on to rendezvous with Khalid.'

* * *

They could still see the wreck from a great distance as Conor carved his way through the wadi. The crashed chopper looked like some eerie squashed fly outlined on the horizon. When they couldn't see it any more and Lucy was gasping for breath, they stopped.

She could see he was waiting for her to catch up. She realized then she could only walk five kilometers or even less than that. She didn't want to stop, in case he thought she was weak, but she needed to stop, before she was far too exhausted to continue. It was only an hour off from the time of the meeting with Khalid.

Lucy could feel her whole body aching. Those early morning jogs, which had seemed so worthwhile as she plodded through the London streets around her flat, seemed to have been utterly useless. She concluded nothing could have prepared her for this kind of terrain, except perhaps an Army route march.

She remembered his warnings as they were about to leave the crash site. 'Whatever you do, avoid getting lost. Just keep me in your sights. I need to go in front. Otherwise, there's a danger of falling into a gully. I won't be saying much. So don't take it to heart.' He added, 'Keep listening out for any warning from me. If you can't go on, let me know.'

'I will,' said Lucy, with every intention of not holding him up. That was one of the reasons why she'd kept going so doggedly. Another ploy had been to think about both her father and Matt. She alternated, imagining how many times the two of them plodded through the desert. Over and over again, she questioned what had drawn the men she loved like a drug to this forsaken land? And, now, here she was, following in their footsteps?

Many times, she thought about home and the life she'd left behind, but hardly ever about Nick. The journey was proving to be something of a bad dream, but much more painful.

Somehow, she wouldn't have found enough energy to talk to Conor, even if he'd let her. She imagined he was no good at small talk anyway. She needed to keep concentrating in case she lost sight of him in front. Doubtless, he'd be less than happy if she didn't follow his advice.

But she knew that, in spite of his brusque manner, he could be gentle too. At least, he'd shown compassion when he'd checked to see if she had any broken bones. Recalling the incident caused a tiny throb, which almost

51

made her forget her aching muscles. It was the same throb she'd felt when she'd pulled off her shirt in front of him and let him examine her rib cage. She'd squashed it successfully then but, now, it gave her something else to think about rather than her own shortcomings.

As she plodded on, she looked up at the sky. He'd been right about the moon being nothing like the one they saw at home. It was enormous, its great silver eye coldly illuminating her painfully slow progress. It held no encouragement for her because she had no time to stand and stare, no time to muse on its kind beauty. That night it seemed awe-inspiring and remote, far beyond the contamination of human kind, sailing majestically in the black velvet sky, attended by clusters of brilliant star companions.

Sometimes when he stepped into a shadow thrown from tall scrubs or rocks, she was afraid he'd disappeared for good, but that lone black figure, hump-backed under his pack, always re-appeared to encourage her. She spied him in front of her again, waiting silently but, this time, he didn't move off. She realized he was allowing her to catch up.

'Okay? It's time for a break,' he called as she approached, breathing heavily. She saw him unscrewing the water bottle, then he was handing it to her. She found she was gasping for a drink even though it was so cold. She shivered as she felt the cold liquid strike her throat.

'Careful,' he said, 'it's precious.' She handed it back and looked round for somewhere to collapse. The natural choice was a nearby cairn of stones.

She turned and he must have been reading her mind because he got there in front of her. Then he peered at the innocent-looking mound, examining it with his powerful torch. Afterwards, he kicked at the stones, visually inspecting the whole area.

'What are you doing?' she asked wearily. All she wanted to do was sit down.

'I'm checking for snakes and scorpions. They like to sleep in places like this between the rocks. You can find them over here in branches and twigs too. The last thing we want is a bite from either of those buggers.'

His voice sounded as tired as her, but he went on examining the place, his heavy boots assaulting the stones and his gloves turning the smallest over. She stood awkwardly, waiting for him to finish. She didn't offer to help, although she could have. She was well protected too. He made sure of that, making her dress up before they left the crash site. She'd put on his enormous T shirt and anything warm he could find as well as the scarf and the goggles. She looked down at herself thinking she looked both dirty and ridiculous now.

She remembered what he'd told her, 'You

53

mustn't ever put your hands anywhere without first looking to see what's there. That's why you need gloves. It's like you must never go barefoot.' He'd gone on to explain, 'That's why natives in tropical countries walk looking down at their feet. Not because they're feeling less than equal to the Brits.' There'd been a hint of amusement in that, at least.

She'd thought then it would do him good to be funny more often because his was the kind of mouth, that could do with smiling more. He'd added, 'They're looking for snakes. Luckily, we have boots to wear.'

At the time she'd almost giggled, although she hadn't felt like it any more than she did now, because he possessed the unfortunate manner of delivering useful maxims like a college lecture.

As an exhausted Lucy stood, dying to flop down, and watched him patiently checking for creepy-crawlies, it crossed her mind perhaps he didn't know any other way to deliver information. Maybe he wasn't used to talking to women? Anyway, at least he practiced what he preached. What if she'd sat down on one of these rocks and a snake had bitten her? She shuddered.

'Okay, Come over here.' He was settling himself on a large flat boulder, indicating she should join him. She flopped down beside him wearily and he handed her a compo. Whatever he said earlier, the high-energy bar hadn't such a nice taste as a chocolate one.

They munched away in silence. Even at rest, he'd little to say. Perhaps he was as tired as she was? Then she dismissed the thought. He certainly didn't look worn out, but the silence gave her time to think about the other things he'd insisted she'd known. For instance, his other warnings about the wild animals she might be unfortunate enough to meet in the desert.

'I'm afraid there are hyenas and wolves out there too,' he'd said, staring at her. She'd thought he was doing it for cffcct . . . 'But they're mostly interested in eating lambs left behind by their mothers. There used to be tigers, but they became extinct after the forests were felled earlier in the century.'

'Oh, really?' she'd remarked. She'd kept wondering whether he was trying to impress her, or delivering the warnings on purpose just to see her squirm.

She glanced at him now, finishing his compo bar. At least, he was nevcr boring. Anyway, she already knew most of what he'd told her, although she hadn't let on. She remembcred her father talking to them when they were children, telling them stories about the hyenas and wolves, about the Yemen's crazy baboons roaming around, doing damagc to the villagers' crops and destroying trees for fun. She grimaced ruefully, then realized he was staring at her again.

'Are you okay?' She nodded, then sighed.

'I was just thinking about my father spending his whole life out here.' She didn't add she'd never understood why.

'He must have liked it,' replied Conor tersely. 'Have you nearly finished?'

'Almost.' She chewed manfully on, finding she couldn't get her dad out of her mind. What a waste of time it had been spending his whole life in the Yemen, separated from them in London. Perhaps he hadn't known how much they missed him? She was hoping, at least, that he cared, because she desperately wanted to admire his memory as much as everyone else did.

Suddenly, gloomy thoughts took over. She told herself she must be depressed because she was so tired but, try as she could, she was unable to shake herself out of it. Suddenly, the chopper crash was staring her in the face and the remembrance of how Conor buried that poor pilot. He'd been no more than a boy. At least, her father had been old, when he died . . .

'Miss Page?'

'Yes?' She looked startled.

'You should be trying to keep up your spirits. Not depressing yourself.' He'd been studying her miserable face. It was essential to the mission she remained positive.

'How do you know what I'm thinking?' She frowned.

'I can guess. I've been depressed myself and it's no good. Snap out of it.'

'I can't help thinking about the pilot,' she said. 'Don't you feel the least bit sorry he's dead?'

'He was a soldier.' Conor considered his words carefully. It would be no good showing her it really upset him too.

Lucy turned to him, 'You know, he never said a word to me, even when we first set off? In fact, he ignored me totally. At least, I prayed for him.' She sighed.

'I'm sure it was nothing personal. He would have disapproved of any woman going on a mission like this. I expect you know when a girl marries into a Yemeni family; her whole life is in the home. Probably the bloke wasn't used to emancipated women.

'The local girls are trained up as marriage fodder as soon as they can walk. Mind you, a lot of them don't like it.' He thought about Leila. How she'd suffered at the hands of her brutal husband. He continued, 'Most Yemeni men, the uneducated ones anyway, treat women like horses. They break and train them.'

'But the pilot wouldn't have been like that. He was obviously educated.'

'Maybe not, but it's in the genes. He wouldn't be able to understand what you could contribute to a mission like this.'

'Thank you,' she replied. He wasn't sure if

57

she was being sarcastic. He really wasn't trying to be offensive and he was glad she couldn't see his eyes in the dark, which might have given away how he was feeling. She was doing a lot better than he expected . . .

'I'm not saying I agree with that attitude,' he added carefully.

'Glad to hear it.' They were silent for a moment, then she added, 'My father died out here, but I suppose you know that.'

'I heard.' He glanced at her sharply. It was the first time she had volunteered any real information about herself. It was good she was talking to him. It would give her and himself an opportunity to unwind. What happened had been a real ordeal for both of them.

'Although he was an expert, whom everyone wanted to know out here, my mother didn't see it like that. She wanted him back home. I suppose she would have liked a normal life. Whatever normal means. She didn't like him going on expeditions all the time.'

'And he still went?'

'Of course. It was his job. He often asked her to go with him, though, but she had us and her own career. My mother's a doctor. Medical, not a linguist.' He smiled briefly, remembering their previous conversation concerning Khalid.

Lucy thought again what a difference it made to his face when he smiled. She felt herself relax a little after the horror of the past

58

few hours.

What would her mother have done if she had known her daughter had been in a helicopter crash? Lucy preferred not to think about her reaction, but she felt the need to keep on talking about her family. Somehow, it made home seem closer.

'My mother also felt the Yemen wasn't the ideal place to bring up a family.' Lucy grimaced. 'But we often came out here to see my father. I've been familiar with this country since I was that high.' She gestured to explain.

'Is that a fact?'

'Conor,' she began, 'I know you think I shouldn't be here and, honestly, after today, after all the horrible things that have happened, I confess I have wondered if I should have come after all but . . .' the admission was making her realize just how exhausted she was, ' . . . but my mother and I couldn't bear the thought of not seeing Matt again. We're desperate to get him back. It would be like . . .' She breathed in, lost for words.

'Like losing your father again?' His reply was reassuring. 'Don't worry about it. You're doing great and, you know, we'll all do our best to rescue your brother.'

'Thank you.' Lucy nodded. She surprised herself by opening up like that. She was even more surprised at his expression of sympathy. It sounded totally sincere. 'What about you?'

she added. 'Have you any family?'

'Not any more, I'm afraid.' He didn't expand and Lucy wasn't going to pry into the strange answer. She felt somewhat deflated and a little hurt by his obvious desire to keep his personal life private. For a moment, she felt she had made contact with a different Conor.

'And, now, we need to get going again,' he reminded her, shining his torch on his watch. 'One hour and we'll be meeting Khalid.'

Another hour seemed a lifetime to Lucy. She had really never believed a walk could be so hard. Nothing was preparation for this. Not her father's tales, nor her mother's pleadings, nor the warnings from the Foreign Office.

'An hour,' she replied wearily, slipping down off the rock. As she did so, she stumbled. He caught her as she was going down. 'Sorry.'

'That's okay.' The smell of the desert was on his clothes, sand and sweat, but his body was warm on that freezing night. Her head reached to just below his shoulder bone. She couldn't feel his steady hands, that saved her, through his gloves, but she could imagine their strong warmth, because she was as close to him now as when the chopper crashed, and he'd pulled her to safety.

At that moment, his presence meant everything to Lucy. Now, in the cold and lonely desert night, she found herself feeling the same again. She needed human contact so

60

badly. In one mad moment, she knew she wanted to lay her weary head against his shoulder, cuddle into his warm body and rest. Then she came to.

'Sorry,' she repeated.

'I told you, there's nothing to be sorry about. You tripped. Maybe it was your shoelace?' He let her go quickly, then kneeled down at her feet.

She noticed the white dust on his hair. Hers was swathed in a scarf. She put the pair of goggles up on top of the scarf. It was then she realized he wore no protection for his head. Perhaps he had given her his?

She could feel him checking her laces. She wanted to put down her hand and touch him again. She didn't know why, but it was a gut feeling. She didn't because she was nervous.

'You're not wearing anything on your head, Conor. Wouldn't it be better if you did? Are you very cold?'

'Not so you'd notice,' he replied straightening. 'There. Keep an eye on those laces. It could be serious if you fell into one of these thorn bushes. They're lethal.'

'All right. Thank you.'

'All in a night's work,' he retorted, grinning. It was only the second time she had seen him smile fully. The tiredness seemed to have left him. She wished she felt better.

The moonlight washed his rugged face in silver. He was looking down at her. 'We have to go,' he said. A thick curly strand of blond hair had escaped from under her scarf and just the hint of a soft night breeze blew it across her eyes.

Involuntarily, he put out his hand and pushed the strand back in place. Her eyes widened. He knew he shouldn't have done it, but he wanted to.

'Sorry. It was blowing in your eyes,' he said curtly. She didn't reply.

To cover what he felt, he turned to his kit bag and heaved it up. 'Come on. Rest's over.' Next moment, he was checking the compass. She came up beside him.

'Will Khalid be waiting for us?'

'Hopefully.'

'That's good.'

'Yes.' He remembered her weary face, when they stopped and her positive efforts to keep up. She had really done better than he thought she would. No man in his position would have wanted to take a woman along on a hike like this. Now, he, too, was feeling more positive. Barring accidents, they should be at the rendezvous within the hour.

He felt at a loss as to what answers to give to such persistent requests for reassurance. She was obviously feeling vulnerable. Or, maybe, she was letting him know by her determination that her past experience of the Yemen counted. He would never understand the female mind. He wondered how long it would be before he understood what she was getting at. He added, 'As soon as we make contact, we'll radio base and let them know we have arrived.'

'Will Khalid have a radio?'

'Sure to.'

'Then what happens?' asked Lucy.

'That's up to him. He holds the trumps,' he shrugged.

'What do you mean?'

'He's the only one who knows Abdul's movements.'

'Why? Is he so important?' she asked. He considered the question and whether he should tell Lucy. If he did, it would lead to more and more questions he didn't want to answer.

'Let's say his links with Abdul are better than mine. Or any of us. He's from the same tribe.' He decided that was enough of an explanation. It seemed to satisfy her.

'Oh, I see,' she said . . . They were walking along together, which Lucy found much less nerve-racking than alone. He was also talking to her reasonably. Earlier on, his abruptness spoiled any notion Lucy thought of him as being just ordinary. That's a turn-up for the book, she whispered to herself. She felt less stressed. Under an hour to go.

You can do it, Lucy. It was like when you had been somewhere and you were dying to get home . . . 'What are you thinking about?'

His eyes were fixed straight in front of him. She could hear him breathing heavily.

'Lots of things. Matt. My family. Home.' Her own breaths were short, but even. They were almost jogging along together. Her spirits lifted. It was so much better this way.

'And where's that?' he asked. Lucy had already told him about her mother and father. Now she knew he wanted to hear about where she lived.

'Carshalton's my home. Have you been there?'

'Yes, I know it. Surrey. Nice county. Lots of beech trees.'

'Where do . . . did you live?' He looked as if he wasn't ready to tell her and she wondered what he was hiding. Finally, he answered,

'I'm a bit of a nomad really, but my old home was near Hereford.'

'Now that is nice,' she replied, 'I've been there on holiday. I used to go walking on the Malvern Hills.' She realized for the first time since she met him they were making small talk. He was really taking part in the conversation, instead of her volunteering all the information.

Perhaps she would find out what had happened to his family? But, maybe they were all dead and he didn't want to talk about it. Things are looking up, Lucy, she thought, maybe Conor and I might get on after all.

Then, suddenly, she realized the moon

withdrew its light, plunging them into black dark.

'Shit! Sorry.' he added quickly.

'What's the matter?'

'The matter is, Miss Page, we can't see a bloody thing. I thought this was too good to last.'

'So did I,' said Lucy truthfully, glad he couldn't see her face.

'Well, we've been lucky so far,' he snorted. 'We'll have to take the rough with the smooth.' He looked down at the compass, then up to the heavens. Even the stars disappeared. It was the worst thing that could have happened right now, he told himself grimly. Now they were traveling blind in desert terrain. There was no opportunity to survey and memorize the physical features of this wadi. He had expected the chopper to drop them in the appointed place, but he knew there would be ravines.

'Heavy cloud,' he said. He put his hand out and caught her arm. He could feel the heat off her. 'Listen. Whatever you do, keep me in your sights. Fix your eyes on the torch and follow. I have to go first. Like before. Don't wander off. We're in a particularly dangerous part of the wadi. Where it narrows, there could be ravines, which the rains have carved out.'

'I won't. I promise,' she said, as he let go her arm. Lucy experienced a moment of real apprehension as her instincts told her they

65

were losing both physical and mental connection.

She felt a keen tug of disappointment. She was sure she had been close to finding out what made this extraordinary man tick. 'May I ask you something?' She needed to speak to him again.

'Feel free.'

'Why are we meeting Khalid here?' It had been bugging her ever since they took off in the chopper. 'Why didn't he fly to Sana'a or to the Army base?' Conor's torch made a pool of light on the ground.

'Just take it from me, Miss Page, that the high mountains are the best place to meet Khalid.'

'Does he live up there? I thought you said he was a lecturer and a politician.'

'I did.' He answered patiently.

'Well, is he some kind of hermit?'

'Miss Page, I'd rather we got going than I stand here answering unnecessary questions.' Lucy flushed. The moon had gone in and the man she knew and disliked had come out. He was right of course. She was wasting precious time, but she really wanted to know. 'Are you ready, Miss Page? Remember, keep behind me.'

'One more thing,' she said, determined to have the last word, to show his boorishness didn't matter.

'What now?' It was almost a snarl.

66

'I'd be glad if you would be a little less formal. Call me Lucy. It'll save your breath.' He was silent for a moment. Perhaps her sarcasm had hit home.

'Okay, if you like.' Seconds later, she was following the plunging pool of light his torch made.

Everything was going well until Lucy realized she couldn't see the torch any more. What had happened? Where was he?

Then, with a shock, she knew. She had been on auto pilot, like you do when you're in a car and tailing another blindly and you arrive home without your knowing, but this was no English road.

She had been following the will-o'the-wisp torch light blindly, until her mind slipped off somewhere and she'd lost it. She'd been sleepwalking

'Conor,' she shouted, looking round. 'Conor? Where are you? I'm here.' She turned in a circle. It was an eerie feeling, being alone in the inky dark. She tried not to panic. Then she heard a distant shout:

'Don't move. I'm coming.' Lucy was looking for his light. She could see the torch now, jigging up and down in the distance.

'Thank God,' she said and took two steps forward in utter relief. Then the ground fell away under her boots.

He heard the anguished scream reverberate through the landscape. He froze. 'Lucy.' He began to run madly. Then checked himself.

'Slowly, you dickhead,' he breathed. 'If she's gone down a ravine, you don't want to fall too. You have to get her out.' His mouth was dry and he could find no spit to wet it.

Barring accidents, that's what he'd said. He was a Jonah. He should have been watching her closely. He knew how tired she was. She'd fallen asleep on her feet And she was his responsibility. God, he hated his job.

All his experience hadn't prepared him for the way he felt that terrible moment. Then it started helping. The survival text book was engraved in his mind. You must avoid getting lost, falling into ravines, or stumbling into enemy positions . . . If a member of the corps wanders away from the main body . . . He grimaced. Too late for that. Seek out the casualty immediately, but not at your own risk . . . His training was forcing him to be measured, detached, practical. Meeting Khalid would have to wait.

For the umpteenth time that trip, he deplored the fact he wasn't traveling with infra-red night goggles, which would have prevented this disaster.

So he stood motionless, swinging his torch and shouting, 'Lucy, Lucy, can you hear me? Where are you? I'm coming.' He needed to locate the ravine. Only then could he proceed. Inside, it was agony to wait for her response. It might not come. Then he prayed, 'Christ, let her answer. Don't let her die.' He hadn't begged like that for years. He couldn't afford to lose this girl.

Suddenly, the moon came out. 'Thanks,' he said grimly, looking up into its calm, silver face at the same time as Lucy came to, down in the gully.

Chapter Three

Her fall into empty, black nothingness had been even more terrifying than the chopper crash. She blinked as she stretched her arms and legs. She couldn't believe she wasn't seriously hurt this time either.

'Lucy!' The echoing sound carried over, where she lay, and floated across the still landscape.

'Conor, I'm here! Down here!' she shouted back, feeling her legs gingerly, wincing with pain from her side, which still hurt, but, otherwise, she seemed all right. It was a miracle.

She looked round. She had fallen into a steep gully, carved out by some mountain torrent rushing through the wadi. The sides were sheer, smooth rock. Maybe ten meters high? She shuddered, praying the moon wouldn't go in again.

The thought of facing the black night alone

once more was utterly terrifying. Where the hell was he? She shouted again . . .

He was advancing slowly and carefully, taking his time, squashing every desire to run. He was sweating profusely. If she had a broken leg like the pilot, if she was badly injured, he couldn't carry her. He would have to leave her too and seek Khalid's help. That's if he could get her out. Wherever she was.

'Conor.' He could hear the urgency and fear in her voice.

'I'm coming,' he shouted in the direction from which the call came. 'Hold on, Lucy.'

'I'm in a gully. Over here.' She looked up at the moon and begged it not to disappear . . . Meters below him, she was trying to stand up. She tottered a little from shock, but succeeded. She was realizing how much she ached.

It seemed like an eternity of waiting but, then, she caught a glimpse of the dark figure above her, before she was engulfed in a pool of light. She blinked, shading her eyes with her arm. He redirected the torch.

'I can't get out!' she shouted.

'Are you hurt?'

'No. Not much.' She was not going to panic. Relief swept through him. His quick eyes and mind summed up the situation. She had fallen about six meters. Straight down and lucky enough not to have broken any bones or injure her head. If the gully had been a ravine with

70

sloping sides, she could have broken her limbs on overhanging trees, stones and scrub. Even her neck. The downside to this situation was there was no convenient vegetation to attach a rope to.

'Okay, hang on. I'll have you out soon,' he shouted confidently. He took off his kit bag and squatted, looking for his rope. There were no natural anchors which the nylon would adhere to. He needed to find the spike.

Being always prepared for accidents like this, he kept a piton with him, even when he wasn't mountaineering. The spike could be pounded into a narrow crack in any rock and could hold several thousand pounds in weight if seated properly.

He wondered if she could climb with a rope round her, using her own hands and feet to help her. He doubted it. Then he remembered her admission about being able to use a pistol. Maybe Lucy would surprise him again? He could only hope.

She heard him hammering frantically. 'I'm securing a rope,' he shouted. 'Is there any chance you can loop it round yourself and climb up?'

'I can try,' she said. She was thinking about school. How she'd used the climbing rock. Just a sheer brick wall with hand and foot holds. She'd never done it since. She hadn't been very keen, being academic rather than sporty, but she could try, and that was what she was going to do now.

Briefly she thought of their Games master. He'd been a bastard, and she had never believed anything he said would have come in useful in her future life. 'Thanks, O'Dwyer,' she muttered grimly.

The nylon snaked down towards her, hanging from the ring in the head of the piton. He clipped the rope through a karabiner so there would be no danger of it slipping accidentally. She grabbed hold.

'Got it.'

'Tie it round your waist. Make sure it can't come undone. Bowline if possible.' He hoped. She couldn't remember how to do that one even though she'd been in the Guides. She used a triple granny.

'Okay.' She was sure it was secure.

'Right. I'm going to try and pull you up. With your help of course,' he replied. 'However smooth the rock face is, it's technically possible to climb. Ready.' Lucy glanced up at the moon. The sky was clear and the stars looked down. She grimaced at his confidence in her technical skills.

Then the orders came down again, and she was thankful they did. 'When you come up, don't lean against the rock, but stand vertical to a horizontal line. Then you can see and feel if there's any hand hold or foothold. Remember. I've got you if you slip.' She hoped to God she wouldn't. 'Now climb.'

He stood away from the edge, ready to take up the slack as she started. His feet were firmly braced. Any strain on the rope from below would come then directly to his front.

When he could feel her moving he began to take up the slack . . . At one point, Lucy thought she was doing okay. Her toes were slipping and sliding, but then she got a foothold, and the next hand hold.

She was on the face of the gully now, climbing. Once, her foot actually slipped and she was left dangling. She heard him swear out loud with the strain.

Up she went again, and up . . . Sweat swept down from under her hair and rolled over her face, soaking the scarf wrapped round her neck and her jacket, but she was getting there.

As her exhausted face appeared at the top, he leaned back and hoisted her over. A moment later, she was sprawling on the ground. 'Well done, Lucy, well done.' But she couldn't speak. She was totally done in.

He hurried for the water bottle and handed it over. She took a swig gratefully and, when she finished, she looked into his eyes. 'I thought I'd had it, when I fell.'

He couldn't blast her for dropping off, like he would his men. Nor for disobeying. She shouldn't have moved when he told her to stand, but he hadn't the heart. He was only grateful she was alive. She had some nerve and she knew how to climb. He could hardly believe it.

'I thought you had too,' he replied, 'but . . . I'm very glad you're back.'

'Thank you.' They sat together. He could feel her shivering. It was a natural reaction to put an arm about her shoulders to steady her.

She leaned her head against his shoulder quietly and he let her. She couldn't know what he was thinking. All she needed now was comfort. 'Have we missed Khalid?' Her voice was anxious.

'No, he'll wait.' Conor was sure of that. The Arab would not go away until the chopper dropped off its human cargo. If it didn't come, he would wait until someone told him otherwise. Unless he knew they had crashed. It was an ever-present fear in his mind, but he'd find out when he met Khalid. The signal had been agreed. Two minutes before the estimated time of arrival, the guide would start indicating his location and go on doing it. Minutes passed.

'Shall we go on?' whispered Lucy.

'Get your breath back first. It's been an ordeal. You're shocked. Lie down on your side. Here, put this under your head, while I see to the rope.' He handed her a rolled-up sheet of some plastic material.

The torch light withdrew and she lay there watching him, taking out the piton, coiling the rope and stowing it. He came back, 'You were very lucky,' he said softly. 'It could have been a ravine. I mightn't have been able to get you out.' He was standing over her now, looking down. 'Anyway, where did you learn to climb like that?'

'Guess?' she replied weakly, but with a wry smile.

'I can't.' He was at a loss.

'School. It wasn't only pistol practice, you know.'

'Phew.' He whistled. 'Well, if I ever have any kids, I'll send them to a school like that.' They fell silent, both considering what he had just said . . .

'I'm ready to set off again,' she said, ten minutes later.

'Barring accidents . . .' he stopped as if he wasn't going to tempt Fate. 'It's only about three miles now to the rendezvous. This time, we'll walk together. I can't risk something like that happening again.'

Lucy was pleased, because she couldn't bear the thought of trailing behind him and getting lost. She was too scared.

'I wish I had my night glasses with me,' he remarked. She was surprised. It was an unexpected admission he'd forgotten something.

*   *   *

They proceeded in silence. Half an hour

75

passed without event, and the moonlight remained. Lucy remained very close to his elbow. He had slowed down. She assumed he was taking her fatigue into consideration.

'We should see Khalid's red flash light soon,' he said, glancing at his watch.

Five minutes later, an exhausted Lucy and a very tired Conor were standing below the outcrop of rocks that been the agreed meeting place on the map. There was no sign of the Arab.

'Are you sure this is the right place?' asked Lucy.

'Quite sure.'

'Then he must have gone. Or he hasn't come?' She was about to sit down but remembered. Next moment, she was inspecting the crevices around the rock she had chosen. Then she sat down, while he stood motionless staring out at the horizon.

'What do you think has happened?' she asked. He turned. He was not going to tell her what he suspected. That Khalid had not been expecting them to make it. That he knew about the crash.

'I'm thinking while we're waiting, we'll rest and, if he doesn't come for us, search and rescue will.'

'But why isn't he here? He must know how important it is,' persisted Lucy. He went over to her.

'I know you're disappointed but, just as our

76

chopper went down, and you fell into the gully, anything could have happened to Khalid. Nothing can be taken for granted in the desert. We mustn't lose any sleep over it and that's what we need now.'

'Sleep? Here?'

'It's as good as anywhere,' he said, swiveling his torch.

'Then what happens?'

'Search and rescue will take us back.'

'But I can't go back,' cried Lucy. 'What about Matt?'

'I don't mean give up,' he replied. 'By the time we get to the mountain base, we should have heard from Khalid. Then we'll take off to meet him in a vehicle.'

Lucy was trying to control herself now. She could hear that patient explanatory tone, which always annoyed her. She felt raw from her experiences and desperately disappointed. In fact, ready to explode.

'I hate him,' she muttered, knowing how petulant it sounded, but she couldn't help it. Khalid not being there was extremely unsettling, after all the trouble they'd been through. He stopped what he was doing.

'Why?'

'For letting us down like this,' Lucy spluttered.

'Forgive me, Miss Page,' he said, 'but this isn't the place for tantrums.'

Her eyes glared at his back. She hated how

he used her surname when he was irritable. She couldn't have done without him but, at that moment, she couldn't do with him. She was also angry with herself for showing her short fuse.

'Here,' he said calmly, brushing her off, 'this'll do.' Now he appeared to have forgotten she was cross, which made her more so. She strode over.

'How can we sleep here?' she snapped.

'Easily.' He pointed. He pin-pointed a spot under the overhanging outcrop. A broad ledge off the ground. 'And in this sleeping-bag.' He had a satisfied look on his face as he was taking it out from the kit bag. She watched silently as he unrolled it. 'It's pretty big. We'll both fit in it.'

'You must be joking. I can't sleep in there,' she said. He stopped what he was doing.

'Well, you can't sleep out there.' He gestured. 'You never know what's wandering around. I mean it. So I suggest you forget being prudish and accept my offer.'

She frowned. How dare he call her a prude? He started unfolding the sheet of shiny material, which he'd placed under her head earlier. It reflected the moon's silver, as he dragged it into a square on the desert floor and anchored it with stones.

She sat dumbly watching. 'Marker panel. For the rescue chopper. So they'll know our location. While I'm doing this, I suggest you take off your scarf and goggles—and anything else you want—and climb in.'

It was deadlock. Either she did, or she didn't. 'I have to do something first,' she said. He handed over the torch.

'Well, go behind the rocks. Look down before you squat. Remember the snakes.' He was so cool, so matter-of-fact. She went off, with her cheeks blazing.

When she came back, she was cooling off. He took the torch. 'My turn.' Then he walked off in her tracks. It was now or never. She hadn't much option, but she couldn't imagine herself going to sleep. Sharing it with him. No way.

She climbed on the ledge, looked round—he wasn't in sight—took off her goggles, scarf, jacket, boots—and slid inside the unzipped bag. It smelled of him. What was she worrying about? Togetherness with another human being. He was only a man, after all.

She felt a tiny throb of excitement inside, which alleviated her weariness. Nick crossed her mind then. What would he have said if he knew? But she was finished with him. All her life Lucy never imagined she would end up on a rocky ledge in the desert, sharing a sleeping bag with a man like Conor. She thought about the effect he was having on her.

He was a paradox. She couldn't stand him, but she admired him. She hated his attitude, but she kept on forgiving him. Besides, he had

79

saved her life twice.

Then he was coming back. She felt him sit down beside her. She could hear him taking off his boots. Mentally preparing herself for this test of their nerves, she snuggled down inside and lay stiffly on her side, clutching the top of the bag with tense fingers.

She told herself she was acting like a school girl. That lots of women fantasized about situations like this. She was certainly fulfilling lots of female fantasies, but what about her own?

'It's all right,' he said, bending his knees to get in. 'I shan't be taking my clothes off.' He must have seen she had taken off hers. 'I can assure you I wouldn't be doing this, if your kit bag had survived, but it's necessity. Now we've stopped walking, we'll start to feel the cold very badly.'

She didn't answer, just held her breath as he wriggled in and lay with his back to her. He was warm, very warm. It was a very tight fit. She closed her eyes and thought about how he held her when the chopper crashed, how she leaned against him when she'd climbed up from the gully. How he touched her hair, held her hand as they were falling out of the sky.

She would never have believed how much she wanted to snuggle into his back. She remembered sitting behind him in the chopper. That deep, warm tan, those broad shoulders. She shook off the thought. He was breathing regularly. Had he gone to sleep already? So much for her imaginings.

'Are you awake?' she whispered.

'Of course I am,' he muttered.

'Do you think they'll find us?'

'Yes.'

'How long?'

'Three or four hours maybe. Now go to sleep.' He was treating her like a child again, but she wasn't one, and she wanted him. Simple as that. She couldn't believe how much. She didn't know why. Perhaps she was going mad? This wasn't the self-assured image she'd been careful to project. A professional doing a professional job.

She bit her lip. It was probably the desert's fault, being out here with only him for company. Its sheer loneliness made her yearn for closeness. She disliked herself for even thinking about what she was hoping. What an utter fool she was proving to be. Lucy curled up miserably, trying to sleep but, still, her senses were begging him to turn over and hold her.

He lay quietly for a little while, then shifted into a position that put the most distance between them as possible. Which wasn't easy in the confined proximity of a sleeping bag.

But Lucy felt it was a definite gesture confirming what he'd stated earlier, that, if he'd any option, he wouldn't be lying down next to her.

Perhaps she, or he, should have slept in the open. Facing a wolf or a hyena would have been terrifying, but less frustrating. Then she gave herself a good telling-off for being such an idiot.

You're a stupid cow, Lucy, he hasn't any idea how you're feeling right now. He thinks you're a dead loss. He never wanted you along anyway. He's probably got a wife and six kids back home.

She thought of everything else she possibly could to take her mind off how she was feeling. Khalid, Matt, her father, mother, home, but everything swung back to Conor . . .

He lay there, silently fighting every instinct within him. He wanted to turn and take the girl in his arms, to hold her. He expected sex with her would be fantastic. Just the thought of it sparked off his erection. He didn't want her to know the effect she was having. He thought how shocked she would be. Maybe disgusted? She might even get up and run.

So he brought himself into the fetal position, hugging his knees. It wasn't just sex. She was getting under his skin in spite of him being dead set against her. Lucy Page was headstrong all right, often annoying, but full of character and pluck. She wouldn't give up. She stood up to him, and surprised him every minute. He couldn't work her out.

She was a challenge and he liked that. A

woman to be reckoned with. Ten years ago, he would have had the balls to turn round and try his luck with her. He told himself he would have succeeded, and she would have loved it, but he was a different man now. He'd grown up. Too many things had happened in his life and he was lonely. Damned lonely.

He had been in love once and look where it got him. It proved a painful experience in all senses. Suitable women were given a wide berth ever since. Mind you, he'd had his kicks. At thirty-two, he should be looking for the one. Before it was too late. Yet it would never be fair on her. What girl would take him on with his lifestyle? Wandering the world at the bidding of his masters. What security could he give a woman? He could hear her regular breathing. It was good she'd gone to sleep. She looked all in and she wouldn't guess how he was feeling.

He opened his eyes and kept watch. He needed to stay alert for the chopper. Or Khalid. He felt very uneasy about the Arab letting them down.

Some years ago, he would have trusted the man with his life. Now he was not so sure. A lot had happened since the trouble with Khalid's family. Maybe Khalid wanted Abdul to succeed in his enterprise.

Putting the personal aside, he preferred to think the guide and he still shared some loyalties, but his uneasiness persisted. Had

Khalid failed to keep the rendezvous because he believed his old friend had perished in a chopper crash?

The thought bugged him continually as he lay there, back to back with a sleeping Lucy, letting the memories loose in his brain so that sleep wouldn't overtake his numbing senses. He was still hoping Khalid would show up.

At around four, when the dawn was about to break and the desert was coming alive, he was rewarded by the distant sound of a helicopter. They were here. Khalid wasn't.

He rolled over with difficulty. Lucy murmured dreamily and pushed off his leg with a warm, slim foot. He grinned, then, hesitantly, put out a hand and touched her bright, but dusty hair. A moment later, he caught hold of her shoulder gently and shook her. It was the pleasantest morning call he'd allowed anyone for a very long time.

'Wake up. We've got company.'

'Mmmm . . . what?' she said, coming to. 'Oh,' she grimaced. She woke with a hell of a headache and she could hardly move, she ached so much. Then she remembered she'd spent the night in Conor's sleeping bag.

'The chopper's here.' Already, he was pulling himself out. He turned to her, 'Come on. Get your things. Hurry up and don't forget to shake out your boots.'

'For God's sake . . .' She was never at her best in the morning. Forcing her aching body to move, she rolled out behind him and began to collect her belongings, while he ran off to wave the helicopter down some distance away . . .

*   *   *

As the dark green Army chopper hovered above like a huge brooding fly, Colonel Ali trained his field glasses on her.

He pursed his lips and shook his head at the sheer immodesty of Englishwomen. The girl was running about, collecting items of her clothing. He sniffed, Ah, Kendall, you haven't lost your touch then.

Then the pilot relayed his message over the radio. 'No sign of Khalid.' Ali hadn't been surprised.

But it was now a matter of national urgency they made contact with the old fox so that Conor and Miss Page could get underway with their mission.

'Take it down,' he ordered the pilot curtly. Next moment, the helicopter stopped hovering and began to descend.

Chapter Four

Lucy sat on the side of the military camp bed and started to dry her hair. Just to be able to wash it had been heaven, but the arrangements had been primitive . . .

After they arrived in the helicopter, Conor took off for de-briefing by Colonel Ali and she was led to a tent, provided only with a camp bed and a chair on which some clothes were neatly folded.

Feeling desperately hot and sticky, she took off the bullet proof vest as soon as she could. Then, she sat down and investigated the clothes, which turned out to be simple everyday wear for an Arab woman.

She longed to put the garments on, but couldn't bear to unless she washed first. So she continued to sit there and wait for instructions, hoping, but never dreaming, she was going to enjoy the comforts of a shower in the desert.

About ten minutes later, a silent soldier dressed in a long, white robe and wearing an Arab headdress collected her. He led her to a canvas contraption, that resembled a circular windbreak, but which fastened up like a tent.

Inside stood several pails of water, which she soon realized were placed there for her to pour over herself. Her 'shower' proved to be a hit and miss affair. Besides knowing that a hundred or so soldiers were ambling about the site which, understandably, left her feeling a bit self-conscious, Lucy found it difficult to aim the contents of the bucket correctly, without half-drowning herself.

She'd lost her toilet bag and her clothes, when her kit had been crushed in the chopper crash. Luckily, her comb and make-up was still in the holdall, which had been jammed beside her in the damaged seat. Conor had ordered her to leave it behind but she'd managed to wrench it loose before he had dragged her to safety. Lucy was very glad, because it was the sum total of her personal possessions.

At least, she had been provided with a cake of rough soap in the wash tent, but neither sponge nor scrub. Not even a jug to ladle out the water. She decided she would find it far too embarrassing to call out and ask for a flannel. She felt sure the Yemen Army didn't need such niceties.

Therefore, she had no option but to either scoop the water up in her hands or throw the whole bucket over herself at one go. She chose a compromise, having washed her face first and, then, put her head in to wash her hair with the soap. Afterwards, she tipped half of the rest of the water over her, worked up a lather and, finally, threw the remainder over her head and shoulders.

When she finished, she'd discovered the Army's taste in towels left much to be desired as they were extremely large and exceptionally coarse. When she wrapped one around herself, she decided, that they felt like sandpaper and could have served for drying elephants.

When she dried herself, she felt the effects of the rough towel most on her face, which had caught the sun in spite of her efforts with high factor cream. Finally, feeling a bit like Jane in the Tarzan films, she emerged furtively, swathed in the voluminous towel, with her dirty clothes over her arm. In spite of all her niggles, to feel hot and sticky no longer was absolute luxury, and to feel clean again was bliss.

Just as she was ready to bolt for her tent, she was surprised by Conor, who seemed to appear from nowhere.

'Feeling better now?' he asked, his eyes flicking over the ugly, green towel from top to toe. Lucy felt particularly sensitive about the way she looked swathed in the monster. He appeared to have no worries on that score. He was wearing hardly anything.

'Lots,' she replied. She hadn't caught sight of him since the moment they had landed at the camp. She supposed he'd been busy but, confronting her like that, she couldn't have stopped looking at his body, even if she wanted to.

It was the first time she'd seen him without his shirt. He was stripped to the waist. He hadn't undressed when they'd shared his sleeping bag the night before. She was sure of that because, after she taken off her clothes, she had heard him kick off his boots, and, she supposed, nothing else. Not that she had taken the opportunity to test her supposition.

Conor's eyes were twinkling and she knew he was aware of her appraisal. 'Good,' he said. 'My turn now and I'm really looking forward to it.' He yawned and stretched as she started to walk off, revealing a six pack, which would have graced a body builder.

Later, as she sat in the tent and toweled her hair dry, her mind flicked back to that lithe, lean figure, that gorgeous body. There wasn't an ounce of flesh on him that shouldn't have been there. In fact, he reminded her of one of those hunky models, who were strewn all over the pages of women's magazines.

But Conor was better than any male model. There was nothing effeminate about him. His body looked perfectly smooth, but she knew how hard his muscles were and how fit he really was. He'd proved that when he'd carried her out of the chopper and pulled her out of the gully.

She'd been right about the all-over tan too. His combat trousers appeared loosely belted and, as Conor disappeared inside the wash tent, her eyes noted the deep, bronze color extended well below his waist.

Then she remembered the impression he'd made on her at the airport and how she'd let herself imagine what his body was really like under the thin material of his fashionable suit. She hadn't been far from the truth.

Lucy smiled ruefully. Now, she knew there was more to Conor than just good looks. Those hours they'd spent together before the Army helicopter had picked them up, were partly revelation and partly frustration.

For instance, sharing the sleeping bag. It had certainly been the strangest night Lucy ever spent with a man. She'd realized the necessity for such togetherness but found the whole episode strangely unsettling.

As she toweled her hair vigorously, she decided she didn't want to examine why that should be. She tossed her head back and smoothed her curls off her forehead. When they were wet, the tendrils clung around her face. At that moment, they were plastered to her soft skin. She concluded their stickiness was probably the effect of having washed her hair in cold water with coarse soap.

She searched through her holdall for her small mirror to check how she looked.

A quick glance confirmed her suspicions. It was far worse than she'd first thought. In spite of all the cream she'd put on, her fair skin had caught the sun. She was hoping she wouldn't peel. Suddenly, she was thinking of Conor's deep bronze. How long did one have to be out in the sun to look like a piece of teak?

She felt exasperated by giving way to such

self-indulgence, as well as frustrated. For God's sake, Lucy, she told herself, you're here in the Yemen to rescue Matt, not to agonize over how you look or whether you've caught the sun or not.

Luckily, a further rummage through the bag revealed a tube of after sun cream. She was thinking of Conor again as she applied it. She was sure, that unlike her, he didn't spend his time agonizing about trivialities, but she sensed he was worried. She had seen it in his eyes. What made him so anxious?

She realized Conor was practiced at hiding his emotions, but not all the time. She remembered his arrogant attitude and his growing irritation at her persistent questions. The man was mercurial. He was extremely quick to let her know he needed to be always in control but, then he could be patient, if he felt it was necessary to calm her down.

She concluded even though she didn't like his arrogance, it had still paid off. After all, without him, she would probably be dead by now.

She had no illusions about Conor putting her in the picture as to what was likely to happen. He wouldn't. Yet, if the two of them were to act as a team, she needed to know. He'd told her twice already they might be shot at. She thought ruefully it would be nice to know who was going to do the shooting before they set out again.

She remembered with a pang how, just once, she and Conor seemed to have connected. The moment hadn't lasted and it might never come again. She asked herself why then, suddenly, she found herself wondering if he was working on some hidden agenda.

She stopped putting on the cream and stared into the mirror as she considered this new thought carefully. He'd behaved very strangely about keeping the rendezvous with Khalid. Absolutely nothing would have prevented him meeting the guide.

He'd given her good reasons for leaving the crash site but, even then, she'd suspected, if she'd insisted staying with the crashed chopper, he would have left her behind without a qualm. She wouldn't even have had the pilot for company, because he'd buried him. And he'd done it so calmly.

No, she decided, evidently meeting Khalid had been the most important thing in the world. She supposed he was only obeying orders but, she realized that, from the very first time they'd met, Conor wasn't at all keen on risking his life to save her brother. He'd certainly resented taking her on the trip with him. He hadn't said so openly, but he'd made it quite clear he was opposed to the idea. Which made her very angry and made her feel like some bimbo, rather than a professional woman who'd known what it was like to live in the Yemen, practically since she'd been able to walk and talk. Her father had seen to that.

Lucy felt rightly indignant then. She put the top back on the cream and smoldered. Her father had led an amount of expeditions into the desert, one or two of which turned out to be of global importance to the world of archaeology. Matt was just as bright. 'witched on', his university supervisor called it.

Who was Conor Kendall to judge whether Matt had been right or not to investigate that shrine? He was just a civil servant. She felt extremely irritated as she mulled over all the possibilities, so she put away the mirror that was never going to provide her with the right answers.

*   *   *

A few moments later found Lucy stretched out on the narrow camp bed with a damp towel covering her and another under her head, staring up thoughtfully at the billowing khaki of the tent roof.

Suddenly, she was conscious of a long shadow, which was thrown through the crack in the tent flap on to the canvas roof. There was someone outside. She sat up and pulled the towel round her.

'Lucy? May I come in?' It was Conor.

'Just a moment,' she replied, stalling. She threw off the towel and scrambled into the clothes some thoughtful person had left

93

hanging over the camp chair beside her bed. Once she'd put them on, she realized the spotless, white, high-necked shirt and pair of cotton trousers were far too big, but she had nothing else to wear.

Hitching them up, she grabbed the comb and mirror, and began to untangle her unruly hair, trying to coax it back into some kind of decent shape. She scrutinized her face, which was rosy red. She grimaced. Why did she have to look like a lobster, when she had to face a tanned Conor, who remained the epitome of cool?

*   *   *

As he waited outside Lucy's tent, Conor wondered how he was going to broach the painful subject. Since his de-briefing after landing, he'd been in communication with London. The conversation with the Junior Secretary, Julian Smythe had been short and to the point.

'For Christ's sake, Julian, let the girl off the hook,' he snapped.

'I might not be your direct superior, Kendall, but no one speaks to me like that. Don't think I won't pass it on,' the other huffed.

'You can puff all you like, Julian, but I intend to make it back to Sana'a in one piece. You realize that will be much less likely if I've

94

a female trailing along, which could mean goodbye to the whole operation. You can pass that on to the Boss.'

Conor decided to put Lucy in the frame. It was the only ploy that might cut any ice with the powers-that-be. Any suggestion that the mission could fail, owing to her unsuitability, might produce results.

He grimaced at what he'd gone on to say and what had finally ensued. From then on, he wouldn't be Julian's favorite person, but he couldn't care less, he was used to going too far. They couldn't do without him.

His outburst was in vain. They wouldn't even consider it. Lucy Page was on the case and there she would remain. Her pig-headedness had evidently made some impression in the Office. They added they'd warned her of the risks and the message for him came through clearly, 'It won't look good if you lose her, Kendall, so make sure you don't. Miss Page has been briefed. She knows the score, while we have confidence in you completely. There's no way you're not taking her unless, of course, she changes her mind.'

He snorted as he squinted up at the sun and, roughly, toweled his hair dry. He was mad, not only because he was the poor bastard, who was trying to pull off a seemingly impossible task, but also because he didn't see what she could be doing inside her tent, that was important   enough to keep him standing outside for five minutes. He was not known for his patience, except when it was absolutely necessary.

'Come in.' A moment later, the flap was thrown back and he found himself looking down at the slip of a blonde, angelic in all-white. Who would have thought she'd have proved to be such a handful? She was almost as stubborn as he was. How the hell was he going to persuade her to change her mind? He wasn't in the best of moods after being half-drowned in that shower and being kept waiting. He particularly didn't want to upset her, especially when he was going to broach the unpleasant subject of leaving her behind.

'At last,' he muttered sarcastically. Lucy glanced at him quickly and smiled.

'What's funny?' he asked irritably, watching her go over to the bed. Evidently, her clothes had been made for some Arab girl, twice her size but, surprisingly, the effect of two sizes too big, made her look smaller, vulnerable and even more attractive.

'Sorry,' she said, turning, 'I was just thinking about the shower. Not exactly five star, was it?' He didn't feel like smiling, but he couldn't help it. He took the wet towel from round his neck and slung it expertly out through the tent flap.

'No, but that's the Army for you.' He'd gained plenty of experience of being on exercise, but he wasn't going to let Lucy know about it. She thought he was a pen-pusher from Whitehall.

'Well, at least, I'm clean again,' she replied, plumping down on the rough Army blanket, then perching there cross legged. She indicated the chair. 'Are you going to sit down?'

'Thanks.' He was close enough to feel the heat of her body. The same way he'd felt it all through him last night. He remembered how she pushed off his leg with her foot, which displayed the tiniest vestige of rosy nail varnish clinging to the toe nails.

Suddenly, he realized he had begun noticing every little detail about Lucy Page. He wasn't sure why.

'Well, why are you here?' she asked. He heard the sarcasm in her voice as he settled his back against the hard chair, its back scoring his sore skin. He was still feeling the effect of the crash, besides the fact he had lent some of his protective garments to her.

He noticed that in spite of it, she'd burned. 'You've caught the sun,' he remarked. 'You really should protect yourself more.' He could see by her expression she didn't like his criticism. He hadn't meant to be rude. He was only pointing out that in a country as hot as the Yemen it was easy to burn badly if you didn't take proper precautions.

Lucy glowered. 'Do you think I'm that

stupid? I put on lashings of cream. It's because I'm so fair-skinned and because we were out in the sun so long.' An awkward silence followed. Then he added helpfully,

'I suggest you do what the Arabs do. Muffle your head and neck up from now on. I'll see if I can get you one of the soldiers' headdresses.'

'Make sure it isn't as big as their clothes then,' replied Lucy tartly, 'otherwise I shan't be able to see where I'm going.'

He smiled grimly. 'I think those clothes suit you,' he stated. Her eyebrows lifted in surprise.

'You asked why I was here.' He considered the best way to begin what to say. 'Well, it's about the trip.' Her eyes held his steadily.

'That's good, because there's a few things I'd like to get straight too before we set off again,' she replied. He sighed inwardly. Their conversation would always be at cross purposes until he came clean.

'I agree.' He considered the best way to begin. He was used to giving orders and, when he spoke to men, they listened and responded. Grey areas were the most difficult for him. He wanted to soften the blow, but he wasn't quite sure how. He put it down to not really understanding the way a woman's mind worked. Lucy Page was extremely intelligent and didn't take to being ordered around.

'Good,' she said, uncrossing her legs and supporting herself on her elbows. As he prepared himself for the task, his eyes kept flicking to the way the thin, cotton shirt accentuated the tips of her breasts, revealing the dark circles about her nipples.

He found it was putting him off, so he got up from the chair and stared around at nothing to get himself back on track. 'That seat's damned hard,' he said, to cover his confusion. He turned to her. 'Lucy, I've something to say you won't like . . .'

'Sounds serious . . .' she interrupted.

'How did you feel when the chopper went down?'

'How do you think? Bloody scared.' She frowned.

'And . . . when you fell in the gully?' He knew he was making a balls-up of the conversation and he cursed himself for it.

'What is this? Twenty questions? How would you have felt? In fact, how did you feel?' she snapped, jumping up.

'Terrified.' Lucy stared at him as if he was joking.

'Why?' She approached him.

'Because . . . I thought you were a goner,' he said sincerely.

'Oh?'

'And I was supposed to be looking after you.'

'Oh, I see,' she said sarcastically. 'You would have been failing in your duty if I'd broken my neck.'

'That's not fair,' he replied. They were

99

facing each other now. Suddenly, the tent seemed unbearably hot. He could feel the perspiration bursting on his forehead and trickling down on to his naked chest.

She was perspiring too. Her blond curls hung in tantalizing tendrils about her rosy face. He should get her a headdress. Pronto, but, maybe, she wouldn't need it?

He put out his hand and touched her shoulder. She was quivering. 'Look, we keep getting off on the wrong foot. I don't want to upset you but—what I'm trying to say is—it wasn't any picnic yesterday and it's going to get worse. I've managed to protect you up until now, but I don't know if I'll be able to afterwards . . . I mean . . .' he struggled for the right words. 'I mean when the balloon really goes up. When I said we might be shot at, I meant it. What I'm asking you is would you consider staying behind?' He swallowed and let go of her shoulder.

She stood motionless, all the energy his touch had evoked, began draining out of her. He wanted to leave her behind. In fact, he intended to. He had made it quite clear he thought she wasn't up to the trip. She felt hugely disappointed.

She could feel hot tears stinging the back of her eyes and she blinked quickly to prevent herself from crying. It was so unfair. The chopper crashing had not been her fault, neither could she have extricated herself from the seat. Falling in the gully had been a pure accident.

But, as she tried to justify past events and her unfortunate involvement, a nasty little voice inside was whispering she knew she wasn't really up to it. She hadn't been strong enough to struggle free from the seat and falling asleep on her feet wasn't too admirable.

Suddenly, Lucy couldn't bear it. The whole of her life over the last few months had been wrapped up in making it to the Yemen and grasping any opportunity that arose in the quest for her brother. Now, Conor was asking her to disregard all those months of pain and effort and using her obvious weaknesses as an excuse to oust her. It was so unfair and she wasn't going to stand it.

'I can't,' she said, forcing herself to reply calmly. 'I can't stay behind. I have to go.'

'For God's sake, why,' he asked tersely. 'Why can't you leave it to the professionals? Do you want to get killed?' He was trying to control his anger, which was directed at himself rather than at her stubborn refusal. He cursed himself for his inability to communicate to the girl how dangerous it was out there, how much he didn't want her to go. Besides, he didn't want to frighten her.

'No, I don't want to get killed. I want to find Matt and both of us to come back safely.'

'But I can't guarantee it,' he replied miserably.

'I'm not asking you to,' she replied quietly. 'I knew the risks before I came here. My mother didn't want me to go either . . .' She was thinking exactly what they said to each other and how painful their goodbyes had been. '. . . but I insisted. I'm rather stubborn, you know. I'm not a person who can just . . .' she was trying to find the right words that would show him how she really felt, ' . . . just sit and do nothing. I can't bear it. At least, like this, I'm giving it my best shot.'

She swallowed and smiled weakly. 'I'm afraid I wore the people down in your office. In the end, they were glad to get rid of me, but I love Matt and want to see him again. Whatever happens?

'You know, I never got to visit my father for ages. Then he died and I never saw him again. I suppose you think I'm being stupid and sentimental but . . . I really do need to talk to Matt again.' She hadn't meant to spill out how she was feeling, but once she started she wasn't able to stop.

Anyway, she seemed to have made her point. Although his face was an impassive mask, she could see his Adam's apple working in his throat.

He nodded in response, biting his bottom lip. Then he put up his hand and wiped the perspiration from his forehead. He could see that her lovely eyes were glittering with unshed tears.

'I understand,' he said and meant it. The way Leila died had meant he hadn't been able to save her either and he would have given anything to have been able to. All his physical strength had been useless and, now, it could happen all over again.

But, looking at her face, he realized Lucy couldn't be persuaded to stay behind. So he knew he must manage to get both her and her brother home safely.

Suddenly, he was feeling something he hadn't felt for a long time and which he hardly recognized. Respect for a girl half his size, who put her case so simply but so eloquently.

He knew he was hard. He'd made himself tough, so that he could cope with battlefield conditions. He'd been at the sharp end. He knew all about men being weak but, also, how, when they worked as a team, they could pull anything off. It took a great deal for anyone to earn his respect.

When they'd first told him he would be taking a woman with him on the mission to Abdul's mountain hideout, he'd been choked with anger at the stupidity of it all and raged about it privately.

If his buddies found out, they'd rag him unmercifully. Call him a baby-sitter and tell him he wouldn't have a cat in hell's chance of fulfilling his orders with her tagging behind. He'd respond in the usual fashion, kicking off, growling about what a bloody, stupid female

103

the woman must be, and how much he didn't care if she got her head blown off.

But he wouldn't have meant it. He abhorred the idea of women on the front line and the confrontation with Abdul was likely to be just that.

He'd always felt women should be protected, although he'd never have said so openly. Since Leila's death, he'd managed to repress that kind of feeling quite successfully on all the missions he'd undertaken.

But, now, he'd met Lucy Page, whose stubbornness of will equaled his own. Although she was no soldier and hadn't been tested to the utmost yet, he had a grim suspicion she would display as much courage on the rest of the mission as she had since the chopper crashed.

She deserved a chance. He hadn't been willing even to contemplate allowing her to sacrifice herself until the present moment. Now she'd explained her reasons, who was he to prevent her? But her sheer determination and daring was giving him an even greater incentive to make sure they'd all survive.

He looked down at her. 'Okay,' he said simply. 'You win. I'll take you.' He didn't add he would anyway. 'But, this time, you have to obey me.'

'Obey you,' she repeated.

'Yes. You have to do everything I tell you. Or none of us will make it back.'

'I will,' she said. He glanced at her sharply. The tears were replaced by a mischievous glint. She lifted her head and stared him out boldly. 'I promise. I won't hold you to your promise of getting us back either.' She was making fun of him.

'It's no joke, Lucy,' he warned. Next moment, to her enormous surprise, he was holding her firmly by the shoulders, his face close to hers. 'You're getting to be quite a handful,' he said, releasing her. It was then he realized he was shaking a little. Quickly, he made for the tent flap.

She flicked back her hair and swallowed. His lightning gesture unnerved her slightly but, although he'd invaded her space, she sensed it wasn't threatening. In fact, she found being imprisoned in those strong hands exciting. For one brief moment, she thought he was going to kiss her, but she dismissed the idea as ridiculous. Then he was pausing.

'I'll see about that headdress,' he said, to cover how he was feeling. He knew he was very near to kissing her lips and also he wanted to very much, but it would have been the worst thing he could ever have done.

Their relationship had to remain on a detached footing, otherwise the whole enterprise could be put in jeopardy. She needed to know he was in charge and he intended to repress any feelings for her. To get involved with her personally at this stage could be very dangerous.

It was then he realized this was the first time he'd contemplated getting involved with any girl seriously since Leila died. The realization shocked him. To cover his emotions, he added gruffly, 'We'll be leaving in a couple of hours. Around dawn.'

'Oh, wait a minute, please.' She was following him. 'Was there any word from Khalid?'

'Yes,' he replied. 'We fixed a new rendezvous. Don't worry, we're taking a Land Rover.' Her face lit up.

'No more walking?'

'No more walking,' he said.

'Thank you for telling me.' Her relief was evident.

'My pleasure,' he replied. 'Now try and get some sleep.' Next moment, he was diving through the tent flap.

When he'd gone, Lucy found her body was still tingling all over from his touch. To calm herself, she prepared a few things for the journey to come, then went over to the bed and lay down.

She shook her head as she stared up at the canvas ceiling, where the strong wind was trying to tear the guy ropes loose with its hot, sandy fingers. Her mind was still reeling from the effect of their conversation.

When she'd first met Conor, she'd decided they would never get on. What had changed her attitude? She had to admit now there was something. Her companion was proving to be even more of an enigma than she'd first imagined. As she began to know him better, she realized more and more there were very good reasons for his behavior.

If only he'd the ability to explain them to her. But at least, he seems to be trying now, she told herself. She thought about his words. He'd said both their lives could be in danger. She admitted such a warning ought to be a powerful deterrent, but was that the only reason he wanted to leave her behind?

She was sensible enough to realize his desire to thwart her cherished plans couldn't have sprung from mere petty dislike of having a woman around to cramp his style, or to make the expedition more difficult for him. No, it went deeper than that.

Her senses were telling her unmistakably, that his body language, as well as his words, were evidence he was frightened of something awful happening to her. In fact, he was so scared he had done his very best to put her off. Admit it's quite flattering, she told herself. He'd been trying to keep his distance, but he couldn't. She only wished he'd been able to be more open with her at first, but, then, he was a man—and a tough one. He probably didn't know how to explain his feelings.

Suddenly, Lucy's conscience started whispering things she didn't want to hear. Was she being selfish insisting on going? Would it have been better if she'd let him go on alone? Was she a liability? She began to feel extremely worried then, she might be doing the wrong thing but, all of a sudden, adrenaline started to replace anxiety. A feeling of real excitement began to trickle through her, making her whole body tingle. Goosebumps started on her legs. It was quite clear what was happening. She couldn't wait to be all on her own with him.

She felt confused and annoyed with herself. Wasn't finding her brother and rescuing him more important than mooning over Conor?

The word evoked the great white moon, which watched over them in the silent desert night, and its millions of accompanying stars. She remembered how she'd felt when, thrilled by their beauty, she'd stood by his side.

Closing her eyes, she told herself whatever the outcome of the mission—successful or not—she'd been right in deciding to go. She moistened her lips, which had gone dry with pure, raw excitement.

She knew the prospect she was facing was dangerous but, in spite of that, being with him was an experience she'd never be likely to forget. She savored the idea of the two of them out there together.

Her life in London had been ordered and uneventful, until she'd decided to fly out to the

Yemen. Now it was fixed on a different star. She'd chosen her course and her instincts were telling her she wouldn't t regret it.

Before she drifted off to sleep, some lines from Shakespeare she'd learned at school came suddenly into her head: There is a tide in the affairs of men, which taken at the flood, leads on to fortune.

'And women,' she murmured. It was her time now . . .Within minutes, Lucy was asleep and the strong desert wind tugging at the tent ropes was not half as wild as the images, which were conjured by her dreams. She tossed in her sleep as she re-lived the times she and Conor had shared. Moments both dangerous and sweet.

*   *   *

After Conor left Lucy's tent, he went off to find Ali in order to persuade him to provide the best vehicle available for the mission. The ensuing conversation didn't prove to be at all easy. It was what he expected.

The Colonel regarded him in the philosophical manner, native to all Arabs. 'My dear Conor, in spite of all the reasons you've been throwing at me, given what I know of your brief, I don't feel able to waste Army resources in such a cavalier manner. Of course, you may have a suitable vehicle for your purposes but both you and I know that,

Allah forbid, there is a strong possibility neither you nor Miss Page may return to us.'

His eyes narrowed as the commander continued, 'Naturally, I pray this will not be the case, but I have a duty to the Government to preserve our Army's equipment. The vehicle I intend to provide you with is entirely trustworthy and well-experienced.' At that point, his eyes glittered. 'In fact, I have used it often myself in the past. It is expendable.'

'Like us, you mean, Ali?' snarled Conor, ready to fight for what he wanted. 'Look here, you and I have known each other a long time, and been through a lot together.'

The Arab lifted his eyebrows, 'Very true.'

'And both of us came through it. We're still here. This mission will be no different.'

Ali yawned in a bored manner at that point and Conor swung round on him angrily adding, 'Just make sure you're there to back me up when I need you. Or you'll have some answering to do. I've done a lot for your damned country. So have the Pages. They're important people back home.'

Conor knew it was the only thing that cut ice with Ali. Bad publicity was not what the Yemen desired. They'd had enough of it over the last few years. He continued harshly,

'And if you don't pull out all the stops, your government will be spread all over the world press again. I can tell you your foreign donors won't be quite so forthcoming with their aid if

Abdul tops the lot of us,' he added, knowing straight talking was the only way to get through to the wily commander.

'I am sure that will not happen,' replied Ali suavely, 'especially in that your fate remains in the hands of our good friend, Khalid. You and I both know he will hardly let us down, given his personal involvement. If anyone can persuade Abdul to release his prisoner, he can, and then coupled with the promises you yourself carry . . .' Ali made a throat-cutting gesture, 'you can strike.'

At the end of the conversation, the two of them were talking compromise and, finally, a bargain was struck. The ancient Jeep was to be replaced by one a little less elderly. A sophisticated two way radio would be provided as well as the replacement of all equipment which had been lost in the chopper crash.

And Conor even managed to secure the promise of new kits for both Lucy and him, which included the small item of two military headdresses He concluded afterwards Ali proved to be a softer touch than Whitehall, who were less than generous most of the time.

After his call on the Colonel and a lengthy inspection of the Jeep he'd successfully winkled out of him, he went back to his tent and started poring over the maps, consulting the directions laid down by Khalid.

Earlier on, when he heard the tone of

urgency in the Arab's voice above the crackling of the Army radio, he'd been sure this time they would meet. Barring accidents.

'And the quicker the better,' Khalid added, 'because time is running out for young Dr Page.' Conor's mouth went dry as he listened. 'There is no guarantee the Englishman is still alive.' It was then he'd thought about Lucy, sleeping peacefully in her tent. Would both their efforts be all for nothing because they were risking their lives unnecessarily? The girl's dream about rescuing her brother could soon become a nightmare.

Conor knew, like Ali's ancient Jeep, he was entirely expendable. Whatever he did, however successful he was, wouldn't gain him any credit. Only make him more likely to have to do it again. The only thing that mattered to him up to now was his pay packet. If a bullet got him, he wouldn't even end up as a name on a war memorial. In his job, it was up to him, and him alone, to get out safely. Over the last ten years, he had been faced with similarly daunting prospects, but it didn't make things any easier.

Later on, as he lay down on his narrow bed, hoping to snatch a few hours of sleep, he puzzled about what those ten long years had meant to him personally Not a lot, he concluded. Then he thought of her. This time must be different.

Then, carefully and professionally, he forced the memories out of his head, because recrimination and regret were not ideal companions to take along with him on yet another mission.

Some hours later, when the star-filled night was slipping into an icy, red dawn, Conor stood outside Lucy's tent. She didn't answer, although he'd called her softly three times already.

Finally, he looked in through the tent flap. When he saw she was still asleep, he entered quietly. He was glad she had taken his advice to get some rest. Later on, she mightn't get the chance.

He breathed in deeply as he looked down at her, her face, obscured by a mass of tousled curls. He noted her breathing was both regular and easy. He grimaced.

How peacefully would she sleep if she knew what they were really facing? He was sorry he had to wake her but it was entirely necessary if the two of them were to keep the vital rendezvous with Khalid.

He regretted he couldn't reveal what was to be his real part in the mission, but it had been her personal choice to come. He sighed and, putting down his hand touched her shoulder lightly.

'Lucy, wake up,' he said. She stirred, then, startled, opened her eyes and stared into his. 'Wake up.' He took his hand from her shoulder. 'I've brought the transport round. It's time to go. We have to hurry.'

Chapter Five

Ten minutes later, Lucy was pulling back the tent flap. She came out, blinking sleepily, into a rose-colored world where the escaping dawn painted the eastern sky boldly with wavy streaks of red-gold, blue and purple, before the sun took over.

Lucy was always fragile when she first woke up, especially when she lacked sleep, but she couldn't help but gasp at the beauty around her. She squinted up at the golden orb, that was about to climb from behind the looming black mountains and splash the desert with a beauty its harshness hardly deserved.

The air was cool and the slightest of winds breathed on Lucy's forehead bringing her a welcome breath of freshness, which was lacking in the cloying atmosphere of her tent.

She gasped again as she caught sight of their transport. She'd expected the Jeep would be fairly comfortable, but it looked just the opposite.

Their vehicle was a battered-looking, sand-spattered green and khaki beast of a certain age. It was not a bit like the smart four by four vehicles seen on television adverts, or even anything like those shining Land Rovers that were paraded in rows outside the smart car showroom in Central London and situated near to her university department.

And leaning against the battered bonnet was the rangy figure of Conor, dressed in a long-sleeved sand-colored shirt and trousers, covered by a camouflage flak jacket. The effect of the outfit was to blend him into the barren landscape, which the full sunrise was already turning from a wonderful, warm pink into harsh brick-red.

As she approached, the expression on his face gave nothing away. It was as if he hadn't even noticed she was there. He seemed to have been transported into the world of his own thoughts, which Lucy assumed could not have been particularly pleasant, because she thought he looked exceptionally surly.

'Good morning,' she said. He looked up quickly, as if he was trying to shake himself out of his mood. His first sentence only confirmed her fears.

'What's up?' he growled, without even returning her greeting. He must have noticed her own expression was less than admiring as she stared at their transport. She was probably struggling for a complimentary description and failing to find one,

'Nothing, except it looks a bit . . . a bit ancient,' she concluded.

'That's because it is. The Defense

Department isn't going to waste its best vehicle on low priority expeditions.'

'I got the impression we were a little bit more important than that,' she remonstrated icily.

'And who gave you that idea?' he retorted caustically. 'Hostage-taking is common in this country. However important the victim is.' He felt irritable, too.

Although he'd managed to snatch a few hours rest, he was still missing one whole night's kip, when he had been watching over her in the sleeping bag and waiting for search and rescue. Although it was nothing unusual in his job, it didn't make a bloke feel any better. Especially with all he had on his mind.

Lucy winced inwardly at his sarcasm. She was hoping for a mite of sensitivity after their last encounter, but it didn't seem to be forthcoming. She sighed, but didn't alter her expression.

'If you say so.' He glanced at her sharply. The only sign she had taken his remark amiss, was she was scraping the sand into a mindless squiggle with the toe of her Army boot. He concluded his earlier conversation had struck home. Although he'd warned himself to pick his words with her more carefully, he didn't find it easy. The same went for big white lies.

There was no way he could have explained the real reason why Colonel Ali provided them

116

with such an old boneshaker. What would she have said if he informed her the commander was a shrewd operator, who decided it wasn't good economics to provide them with a new Jeep, because it might end up being blown apart by a rocket, launched from some hillside hideout.

Conor would rather have travelled to the rendezvous by chopper. It would have been more comfortable for Lucy, but it would have been far too dangerous, because the terrorists were bound to have an excellent vantage point from their mountain village. He knew what they'd do when they saw an Army chopper. They'd immediately alert their men on the ground to deploy a rocket launcher and blow it out of the sky.

Driving a camouflaged Jeep, he and Lucy were less likely to be spotted initially amongst the scrubby bushes and vegetation. He hadn't told her either, once they met Khalid, they'd have to continue the last part of the journey to Abdul's hideout at night, and on foot. However, if the worst did happen, it couldn't be laid at Conor's door. Although that would be little consolation.

But Conor had no intention of ending up dead. He'd been very thorough in all his preparations. This time he didn't want anything to go wrong like with the chopper. He still suspected the helicopter had been sabotaged, but there was no proof.

117

He and Lucy were facing twenty-five miles of desert and he knew it would not be pleasant if they broke down. The terrain consisted of high ground, leading to the mountains, separated by dry, flat basins of desert.

Therefore, he'd been taking no chances with the Jeep and he'd checked over the vehicle's engine several times personally before he went to bed. He was fully aware of the kind of problems that might ensue if he and Lucy were forced to ditch before they reached the foothills. He told himself he had done all he humanly could to ensure nothing went wrong.

He'd requested a guard on the vehicle after he finished the checkup and, only when the soldiers arrived, gone off to his tent to sleep.

However, there was one thing Conor could do nothing about personally. The weather. If they had the bad luck to run into a sand storm, it could scupper any plans laid for the journey.

He'd seen what sand-laden winds could do to both people and engines. Across the border of Yemen's northern frontier lay the Saudi Arabian desert, which he knew well. Out there, he'd experienced winds averaging one hundred and thirty kilometers an hour even in the afternoon. In that harsh and barren place, major sand and dust storms could be expected at least once a week. Those storms could travel.

He considered the two greatest dangers they

faced on this trip were, first, being shot by Abdul and his men and secondly, to be lost in a swirling wall of sand. Determinedly, he thrust the disturbing idea from his mind. At that moment, all that mattered to him was to get on with the job.

'Come on, then,' he called to her. 'We haven't got all day.' Then he strode off to the driver's side.

Lucy bristled as she hurried over to the Jeep, flanked on each side by silent soldiers dressed in a mixture of flowing white robes and camouflage. Amongst them, a bereted Colonel Ali, who just about managed to nod good morning to her.

Conor was already inside the Jeep, sitting at the wheel. She assumed he was cross about having to wake her and doubtless, he was annoyed she criticized their mode of transport. Then, he leaned over and grasped her hand.

Next moment, he was heaving her up into the passenger seat. Inside, the Jeep was worse than she expected by just looking at the outside. Red, sandy dust was thick over everything and the back was a shambles full of heavy equipment, covered by tarpaulin. His eyes followed hers.

'Well, it's the best I could do in the circumstances. The Yemen Army doesn't run to Bentleys.'

'Spare me the sarcasm,' she replied calmly. 'As long as it goes, it doesn't matter what it looks like.'

'I'm relieved to hear you say so.' He grimaced. 'It'll go, I guarantee you that, but it won't be comfortable. The suspension is crap.' He was rooting about in what passed for a glove compartment. 'Here,' he said, producing what looked like a large tea cloth. 'Your headdress, as I promised.'

She could have sworn there was a malicious gleam in his eyes. She stared at it doubtfully. She no desire to put that on her head. His eyes narrowed.

'You need to wear it. It'll protect you from both the sun and the sand. You don't want to get burned even more, do you?' She shook her head, fiddling with the cloth. 'Here, then. I'll help.'

Next moment, he draped the offending article over her head and began to fix it expertly. She sat there silently, only conscious of the deft touch of his hard fingers. Then, as she emerged from the tangle, with the headdress in place, she caught sight of the expression on Colonel Ali's face, which was half amusement, half exasperation.

'There,' said Conor, evidently satisfied with his handiwork. 'Now, for your goggles.'

'Oh, dear,' she said, looking at them.

'They're essential,' he added shortly, handing them over. 'Put them on.'

'Okay.' She obeyed him. Ever since they'd talked together in her tent and he explained to her about the need to do as he said, she'd promised herself she wouldn't be difficult. 'But where are yours?' she asked to remind him she wasn't the only one who was going to look ridiculous.

'All in good time,' he snapped. 'There's something else.' He leaned over the back, tweaked out the bullet proof vest and shook his head at her as if she was a naughty child. 'Yours, I presume. I don't want to nag, but these cost money. It was a good thing I found it buried in that dirty heap of clothes by the entrance to your tent. You might have lost it to one of Ali's light-fingered lads.' He nodded mischievously towards the Colonel, who responded with a slight salute. Lucy lifted her eyebrows.

'Don't worry,' grinned Conor. 'He'll never know what I think about some of that shower. Seriously, if you left your vest behind, you might have found yourself . . .'

'Full of holes?' interposed Lucy. 'I know. And I'm sorry.' She was about to add, 'I was bound to have remembered it in the end,' but changed her mind at the last minute, because he was looking at her ironically.

Self-consciously, she pushed back an escaping curl from under the headdress, then suddenly giggled. 'I'm sorry to laugh, but I must look like someone out of an old movie. The Desert Song, for instance? Eunice Grayson, wasn't it?' Her mother loved old musicals and had forced her to watch it as a kid. Lucy suspected it was because the film featured the desert, where her father spent most of his time.

'Never heard of her. What about The English Patient?' His eyes were dancing with sudden amusement.

'Okay, what about Maggie Thatcher when she was riding on that tank in the Gulf? You've heard of her, I take it?' Lucy's eyes sparkled as she responded with verve.

His mouth broke into a smile. 'Don't worry,' he said, 'you don't look a bit like Maggie. You look fine.' He was rooting about again behind his seat. 'Now, how about this?' He withdrew an identical headdress and goggles and put them on. She shook her head in amusement.

'I'd say,' she considered jokingly, 'Lawrence of Arabia?'

'Hardly, but you're getting warm.' She couldn't see his eyes now, behind the glasses. 'So, are you ready for the off?' She nodded.

*   *   *

A sudden surge of excitement ran through her body. At last, they were on their way again to find Matt and, even though the rescue was their prime objective, she couldn't ignore the fact she was going to be alone with Conor for the next few hours and they were even joking together.

As she watched him switch on the ignition and heard the engine roar into life, Lucy marveled at the way her thinking about him had changed. He was still just as unpredictable and, often, arrogant but, inside, she knew her opinion of the man was slowly changing. Whether he felt the same about her, she didn't know.

'Ow,' she gasped suddenly, grabbing for something to hold on to as he released the clutch with a jerk and pressed down the accelerator, making the Jeep shoot forward.

'Hold on,' he warned, 'these old boneshakers are no respecters of persons. They need firm handling.'

'I can see that,' she said, adjusting her position as they bumped off over the harsh terrain of scree and scrub.

'By the way,' he added. 'Are you any good at reading maps?' She knew what he was thinking that she was a woman and probably hopeless.

'I might be,' she replied. 'Why?'

'It'll be a help,' he answered surprisingly. 'The maps are back there under the tarpaulin. I studied them earlier, of course, but I might want to check up now and again. If you can read them, it'll gain us a bit of time.'

'Okay,' she replied easily. 'I'll do my best.' She congratulated herself on being so submissive, but found herself wondering if she was going to be able to keep it up. Although she had begun to understand the wisdom behind his constant stream of advice, the old Lucy would have found it practically impossible to obey without question.

However, the dark goggles, which she was wearing, suddenly provided Lucy with a welcome bonus, the opportunity to study him without him noticing. He was certainly expert in the way he maneuvered the Jeep through and over the never-ending series of bumps and hollows, which characterized the rocky plateau on which they were traveling. The twists and turns which he was forced to take were executed in a maze-like pattern.

She saw his knuckles whiten as he fought to keep the aged vehicle under control. Once or twice, she thought they were going to turn over but, besides letting out an involuntary gasp, she stayed quiet.

She remembered how she'd thought the roar of the helicopter's engine had been bad, but the jarring of the old rattletrap in which they were traveling was much worse.

'Horrible, isn't it?' he quipped, turning to look at her. 'What I'd give for power steering.' Then his mouth was set in a hard line again, as he gritted his teeth.

'I'm glad I'm not driving,' she replied. Lucy was having a bad enough time as a passenger. The air was full of sand and grit churned up by the Jeep's wheels and she was very glad now she was wearing the headdress and goggles.

But, in spite of their protection, she felt as if

she'd just visited a less-than-efficient hairdresser, who'd let all the trimmings drop down inside her clothes. She itched unmercifully as the sand penetrated every crevice. It was a thousand times worse than going to the seaside and bringing half the sand on the beach home with you. At least, then you could get rid of it in the bath or shower. Here, it was quite hopeless.

'Do you think riding in this is worse than when we were walking?' he asked. Before she had time to reply, he added, 'I can tell you it isn't. At least, we're making progress.' He was looking at the mileage.

'At this rate . . . barring accidents . . . Sorry, I shouldn't have said that.' He tried again. 'At this rate, we'll be rendezvousing with Khalid about lunch time.'

Lucy grimaced, 'I've forgotten what real lunch means,' she groaned, thinking of how she used to slip out of her office to grab a cheese and tomato baguette, stuffed with lettuce hearts and mayonnaise. Her mouth watered at the thought.

'You think I've brought those compo bars along again, don't you?' The corners of his mouth twisted into a maddening smile.

'Well, haven't you?' She could only hope.

'Never underestimate my powers of persuasion. I'm well in with Ali. Don't worry, I've managed to get two packs of best Army rations off him,' he quipped, with only a flicker of a smile. He needed to concentrate, because driving in the desert was both difficult and demanding, when the sun was playing tricks with the shadows, like it was that morning. He wanted to talk but he couldn't afford to let his concentration slip. If he did, they might end up in a gully like Lucy had the day before.

'Good,' she said, trying to settle her aching back. She was not going to give him the satisfaction of having to explain to her just how horrible their lunch was sure to be.

'Are you okay?' he asked, when he noticed her wriggling in her seat.

'As well as can be expected,' she snapped. 'How do you think I am?'

'Touchy?' he asked sarcastically. She'd thought his bad mood had disappeared.

'No, just uncomfortable.' In fact, she was feeling lousy, but she knew there was no way she could relax in such a murderous old boneshaker.

He didn't speak again for a few minutes. Neither did she. Lucy wondered just how long it would be before he was feeling better and tried to fix her mind on something else. For example, how they were going to free Matt.

She reprimanded herself for not thinking about her brother enough. Not knowing enough about the mechanics of his rescue, but the latter wasn't her fault. Conor hadn't told her. She came to the conclusion the reason she hadn't considered her brother very much over

126

the last few days was because she was afraid something bad had happened to him already.

She couldn't bear the idea that either he'd been hurt or they wouldn't get him out safely so, deliberately, she thrust any thought of Matt aside and returned to her appraisal of Conor.

A sideways glance at his determined profile confirmed the fact he was the best chance the Pages had of getting Matthew out. Even though his moodiness that morning had upset and disconcerted her, she realized that merely looking at his face inspired confidence within her.

She remembered with relief the expert way he'd coped with every dangerous situation they'd faced. She told herself rescuing Matt would be only one more. She was confident he would manage that too, like he managed the Jeep, and Lucy needed to face the fact in spite of her misgivings. He was beginning to handle her too.

The British Consul had been right when he'd said Conor was the best man for the job. Suddenly, she was desperate to find out some more about this man, who seemed able to achieve the impossible. She needed to believe this mission would succeed, but she couldn't ignore the instinctive feeling the coming journey was an excellent opportunity to find out more of the enigmatic Conor's personal life.

At that moment, while he was giving his undivided attention to the wheel of the ancient Jeep, she glanced surreptitiously at him once more.

As they bumped uncomfortably over the harsh terrain, a breathless Lucy found herself wondering how long it was going to take before she truly discovered what he was really thinking. She even asked herself if it would ever happen.

She mulled the idea over and over in her mind as she adjusted her goggles against the sun, which was now full out and burning the scrub and scree around them. Suddenly, Lucy was sure the remedy she needed to replace the confidence lost over the last couple of days, was to earn Conor's whole-hearted trust and admiration.

She realized then and only then was she likely to discover what made the man tick. And today might be the only time she got a chance. Suddenly, she was determined to question him. 'May I ask you something?'

'Fire away,' he muttered. 'But don't make the questions too difficult. I have to keep my eyes on the road.'

'What road?' murmured Lucy. The mountains seemed much nearer now and she thought from a distance, their Jeep must resemble a tiny box on wheels, dwarfed by the giants towering above it. On the scale of nature, his painful negotiation of the sweeping arid area, which spread for miles around and about them, appeared to be entirely insignificant.

'Carry on,' he said, glancing across briefly. She turned her head slightly to avoid the head-on rush of sandy wind. In fact, he didn't want her to ask him any questions at all. This mission was both secret and sensitive, as was his private life. All he could hope for was to turn the conversation back to her.

'What are the chances of getting my brother out alive?' He bit his lip. He didn't want to have to lie to her but neither was he able to tell her the truth. So he went for a compromise.

'I'm not sure,' he replied, 'it all depends on Khalid.'

'Why?'

'You've asked me that before,' he answered steadily.

'And I'm asking you again. What are our chances?'

'If he can set up the meeting . . . if Abdul is amenable . . . There are so many variables. A lot depends on luck,' he shrugged.

'So we have to be lucky,' she said. He thought he could hear a sob in her voice.

'Yes, we do. We've been lucky so far,' he added.

'You mean, like when the helicopter crashed? When I fell down the gully? That was luck?'

'Exactly. You could have been dead and so could I, but we're here, aren't we? All we can do is trust in ourselves and our equipment.' He could tell it was what she wanted to hear. She was trying to bolster her confidence. He would have liked to have said the kind of thing disaster movies were full of: Don't worry, it'll be all right, I promise you. He couldn't.

She was silent for some moments, then she said. 'I'm sorry. I suppose I'm scared.'

'You're bound to be,' he replied smiling, 'but you have to stay positive.'

'Where are we meeting Khalid?'

'That reminds me,' he nodded, 'you can get the maps out if you like. There's a sheaf of them in there. I'll show you. We could do with a break. Just lift up the corner of the tarpaulin.'

'Okay.' Lucy felt better when she was doing something. Just sitting there idly made her feel quite helpless.

She turned and leaning back awkwardly, tweaked off the corner of the tarpaulin. Underneath she could see the maps and further back the hard pewter glint of metal. She pulled out the maps and covered the guns over. She felt shocked. Pistols she had expected, but not a machine gun. At least, that's what it looked like.

And she was sure she was meant to see. 'We're carrying weapons,' she said in a matter-of-fact manner.

'Are you surprised?' He glanced keenly at her and added, 'And your pistol's there as well. I salvaged it from the chopper.'

'Thank you.' Somehow, she couldn't ask him about the machine gun. Maybe there was a rocket launcher in there as well. She'd never seen one and didn't even know if one would fit into the back of a Jeep. She shuddered involuntarily. 'Hopefully I won't have to use it.'

'Hopefully,' he echoed and added nonchalantly, 'and the Ingram is our insurance.' She looked blank and he added, 'The machine gun. M10.'

'I see.' She knew then her earlier suspicions were founded. He wasn't the man the Foreign Office led her to believe he was. How many civil servants did she know who were able to fire machine guns? It was beginning to add up. She only hoped he was as good a negotiator as he was proving to be a soldier but, inside, she knew who she would rather have by her side to rescue Matt.

'Have you done this kind of thing before?' she asked directly.

'What? You mean fire a machine gun?'

'No, I mean getting people out of hostage situations?'

'Once or twice,' he said, 'but I'd rather not talk about it.'

'Official Secrets Act?' She expected the reply to confirm the fact.

'Something like that.'

'Okay.' She breathed in deeply and nodded.

'I'm glad you understand,' he said quietly. 'And it's probably better you don't ask me any more questions about the rescue.'

'You mean you'll tell me when you want me to know.'

'Exactly.' She felt all churned-up inside. What really was his brief? She'd read about men like him. When they left the Service and wrote their autobiographies in the face of Government opposition, they exposed the most horrific revelations as to the nature of their missions. Maybe he couldn't care a damn if he got Matt out or not? Maybe he'd been ordered to do something entirely different? Maybe neither Matt nor she counted at all? Her heart sank.

She didn't speak at all for the next ten minutes, just sat there with the maps rolled up in her lap. He felt worried he'd scared her. The last thing he wanted was a frightened girl along.

Maybe he should have told her more when they chatted the night before. If he'd spelled it out better, perhaps she wouldn't have insisted on coming, but he was bound to secrecy. The die was cast. She only had herself to blame. Years ago, the fact she was scared wouldn't have bothered him. Like him, she would have been expendable. Now it did—and that worried him too.

He felt wretched about everything, as he'd no option but to bend the truth. Now it was too late for her to go back. She probably wouldn't have come at all if he told her what part he was supposed to play in the coming drama.

'You're very quiet,' he ventured. Lucy put her hand up and wiped the sweat and dust from her face.

'I'm thinking,' she said.

'What about?' Here it comes, he told himself. Lucy looked away. At that moment, she would have given anything to grab hold of him, pummel him with her fists, scream at him for letting her come on false pretences then, afterwards, bury her head in his shoulder and console herself in a paroxysm of comforting tears.

But she did nothing of the sort. Instead, she stared stiffly in front of her as if it didn't matter. A moment later, she heard herself saying steadily, 'Well, okay, whatever's going to happen to me, to us, I would have come along anyway.'

He swallowed with surprise. A warm rush of relief ran through him and he felt sudden glowing admiration for her pluck, but he couldn't show it. If he was to affirm her fears, then he might give the game away. He couldn't show her any sympathy. All he could do was try to protect her.

'That's lucky then,' he retorted gruffly. Next

133

moment, he was stamping on the brakes. He indicated the maps. 'Come on then,' he said grimly. 'Let's see if that amazing school of yours taught you anything about map reading.' Slowly and calmly, she began to unroll them.

He showed her the coordinates. 'Abdul's hideout is probably about here. We're meeting Khalid here. He's the only one who knows a way up to the village.'

'Is it on the mountain then?'

'From what I understand it's in a crazy place, clinging to a vertical precipice. Abdul will have chosen it precisely for its vantage point. He'll be able to see us coming for miles.'

'But will he let us up there?' asked Lucy, thinking about the climb.

'Oh, yes,' he replied shortly.

'You seem very sure.'

'I am.' He was not going to tell her why Khalid and he would be allowed to approach Abdul's eyre. Nor why he was the only man for the job. The fact was Abdul asked that Conor, specifically, should be the one to present the British proposal.

If he told Lucy the real reason as to why he was given the job, even if his oath of secrecy allowed it, it would have meant he would have to explain about his past dealings with Khalid and Abdul, and he was not prepared to do that.

They huddled together, looking at the map, each immediately conscious of the heat exuding from the other.

Then, suddenly, he reached out for Lucy's hand. She was shocked, but soon realized he was only pointing her finger at a certain place.

'Okay then,' he said, looking up at her, his mouth only a kiss away from hers. 'Where are we now in relation to those coordinates I just showed you?'

Her brain was working overtime. She didn't want to appear obtuse, but all she could think about at that moment was his nearness. The thought seemed utterly ridiculous given the circumstances they were sitting out in the middle of nowhere, with a machine gun and ammunition behind them, facing probable death.

'Do we have time for a geography lesson?' she snapped to cover her confusion.

'I only wanted to see what else the masters at that school of yours taught you,' he replied maddeningly.

'There weren't any.' He lifted his dark eyebrows, heavy with red dust. 'They were nuns. Except for Games.'

'Nuns, eh? So you're a convent girl?' His eyes mocked gently.

'So?'

'They say they're the worst.' It was Lucy's turn to look surprised but, inside, she was asking herself where the conversation was leading.

'And you're speaking from experience?' she

challenged.

'Don't get me wrong,' he said softly, 'but I've known some very nice convent girls as well.' And, all the time, his hand was still touching hers.

'Have you?' She laughed it off. 'I'm glad to hear it. I can tell you they were all very nice at my school.' She realized with another shock, in spite of the incongruity of the situation and its awful seriousness, she was finding time to flirt with him.

'Do you want these any more?' She indicated the maps. His hand was still brushing against hers and now it felt like a live wire. He was staring at her too and the air felt so thick she could hardly breathe at all. Besides, her whole body was responding to the electricity between them.

'I'm not sure,' he said, 'but we'd better get on. I could do with a drink. I expect you could too.' He was trying to collect his thoughts. Something about those big, blue eyes of hers was strangely affecting and he didn't like it. Although he knew he did really. In fact, he liked it far too much. It must stop.

He shook off the thought he was getting the hots for her. How could he have been stupid enough to bring her along? He should have ordered her to stay behind.

He wasn't happy when his emotions started trying to take over. He had spent the last few years trying to suppress them. They were far too dangerous.

He turned abruptly and began digging about under the tarpaulin. A moment later, he was heaving out the kit bags and forcing himself to remember how much he was against having women with him on the front line.

A few moments later, Lucy was staring in amazement. 'Where in the world did you get that?' she gasped, drooling at the fat piece of melon he was offering her.

'Here.' He thrust the slices into her hand. 'I thought you said you knew about the Yemen. It's a middle highlands melon. I told you I was well in with Ali. He has his own fruit flown out when he's on the job. Grapes, nuts, everything. As well as his qat.'

'But isn't a drug like that dangerous when you're in command?' she asked, her mouth already full of the deliciously cool fruit. She could feel the juice running down her chin, but she didn't care.

'Probably, but they all chew it over here. Ali probably has the best type shipped over for him from Africa, although they grow great fields of it locally. It isn't such a good variety.' She wasn't going to ask him if he'd ever indulged, so she added instead,

'I remember my father talking about how the qat keeps people calm. How it makes them forget their miseries. He said in Ramadan they chew it at night so it makes it easier to fast in the day.'

137

'Maybe we could do with a plug or two,' he joked ruefully, staring at the other less appetizing rations.

'I don't think so,' retorted Lucy. 'I want to keep my wits about me.'

'Good,' he said, packing up the bottles of water into the kit bags. He glanced at his watch. 'Another couple of hours and we should be at the rendezvous. Do you feel better now?' He thought she was holding up well, in spite of the heat and dust.

'A lot, but I'm not looking forward to getting going again,' she said, staring at the dashboard doubtfully.

'Don't say anything in case you put a jinx on the thing,' he said, glaring at the steering wheel. 'I'm the only one who's allowed to do that.' She frowned, hoping he'd elaborate but next moment, he stamped hard on the accelerator and they were off on their crazy way once more.

Half an hour later, Lucy started up from what had been a most uncomfortable doze. She suddenly realized a curse had woken her. That they were slowing down and all around them was inexplicably dark.

'Shit,' he swore.

'What's the matter?'

'Everything,' he snarled grimly. She couldn't see his eyes behind his goggles, but if she had, she would have realized they were narrow slits as he tried to decide on the best course to take. 'Sand storm on the way.'

'What does it mean?' she cried.

'It means we're in deep shit.' He wasn't going to tell her it was the thing he feared most of all, besides being blown away by a Kalashnikov. 'It isn't the best thing that could happen,' was the only explanation he could offer.

'How long will it go on? Should we get out?' Lucy could feel panic rising and fought against it.

'Could be for hours and no, getting out's the last thing we should do. Listen. If we did, we'd get lost. We have to sit out the storm, but we could try and outrun it. There's some natural shelter about a kilometer from here. I marked it on the map. An outcrop of rocks. Probably caves.' He was thinking on his feet now, trying to judge how long it would take, how near they were from the eye of the storm.

The wind was tugging at the Jeep's roof now with urgent, sticky fingers. Conor had experienced sand storms before and they were terrifying. Very soon, the gale would be screaming at them to get out and join it in its dance of swirling death. He needed to make a decision, and, a few seconds later he was stamping hard on the accelerator.

'What are you doing?' she shouted as they shot forward.

'I'm going to race the wind,' he said. 'Hold on tight. The nearer I can get to those caves the better.'

'And what if we don't make it?' she asked, clinging on, battered by the murderous jolting.

'We pray,' he replied grimly, glancing across. 'Just make sure neither your eyes nor your mouth is exposed.' She pulled her headdress close to her face.

'I hope I didn't put a jinx on us. I hope it wasn't me,' she shouted, gripping it tightly, thanking her lucky stars he'd managed to make her wear it and, all the time, the darkness was increasing around them.

'What?' he shouted back.

'Put a jinx on us,' she repeated.

'No, if it was anyone, it was me. Save your breath. You'll need it.' His hands were clamped firm on the wheel as he continued to accelerate, cursing their bad luck under his breath.

The air was so thick now Lucy was finding it very difficult to breathe. She closed her eyes, using her own thoughts as a buffer to cut herself off from what was happening. She could still hear and feel the sandy wind racing all around them. She assumed Conor must have been driving blind and, all she could do at that moment was hang on and pray he was able to find some shelter for them in time.

Chapter Six

The Jeep braked, lurched and, with the most horrible scraping sound she'd ever heard, veered wildly and tottered to the left.

'Hang on,' he'd yelled. 'We're going over!' Next moment, she felt herself being flung sideways. She threw up her arms involuntarily to protect her head but, miraculously, the Jeep righted itself and, after traveling forward for several meters, ended tail up and nose down in the sand. All the time, the merciless wind screamed, making that suddenly topsy-turvy world into a simmering, brown hell.

For several moments after the impact, Lucy's mind was a complete blank. When she came to, she could hear a muffled voice yelling. She didn't know where Conor was at that point, because she was only conscious of what felt like a great weight on her body.

Then she realized it was his weight pressing her down. He must have been flung on top of her. Then he was trying to struggle off. One of his boots was scraping against her leg and it really hurt. In those few awful moments, she didn't have the strength to scream. Then the weight lifted and her whole body seemed to be floating on air.

'Lucy, Lucy, are you all right?' She could hear his voice coming from an enormous distance. She opened her mouth to answer, but her throat felt like it was frozen. *Am I dead?* she wondered.

Then she felt him shaking her gently and was conscious of his warm breath on her face. 'Speak to me for Christ's sake,' he said. She felt words forming silently.

'I . . . I . . .' She was trying to tell him she was all right. Then, she attempted to open her eyes, but her lashes were matted with sand. She put up her hand and rubbed them. It hurt like hell.

'It's all right, Lucy. You're safe now.' She couldn't make sense of the words. 'Come on,' he encouraged, 'we've crashed, but we're okay. I was flung on top of you. You're only winded.' He was running his hands over her body. Dim memories of the chopper crash crowded her brain. She began to cry. Her eyes hurt even more. Then he was pulling at her clothes.

She realized he was trying to get her to move. She couldn't. She just wanted to lie there. 'For God's sake, Lucy, you have to try to get up.' She heard the urgent words, but she was in a daze. 'We need to get to shelter. We're near the cave. We made it. All you have to do is get up and crawl inside.'

She felt him draw back suddenly. Then, she was pulling herself up after him, her hands clawing at anything she could find. She gabbled, 'No, don't leave me.' She found his sleeve and held on tight.

'Okay, okay, I'm not going anywhere. Calm down.' He knew it was shock kicking in.

Then her teeth started to chatter uncontrollably. So he held her tightly until she grew calmer. She could move all right, so evidently she hadn't broken any bones. He tried to cover her face to protect it, but she was terrified. Then he whispered, 'It's all right. It's only the headdress. I'm trying to stop more sand getting into your nose and mouth.' At that point she stared up at him wildly, then buried her head in his shoulder.

Ten minutes later, she was feeling better and able to crawl alongside him into the mouth of the cave. She waited while his torch beam checked the dark recesses and crevices, thinking how lucky she'd been not to have broken anything. The thought of being out here with a fracture made her shudder.

Once he'd got her safely inside, she sat watching him dragging in their supplies. She had neither the strength nor the will to help him. When he'd finally finished, he sat down beside her.

'We were damn lucky,' he said. 'If the Jeep had tipped the other way, it would have crushed us both. Instead it veered along the side of the rocks and tipped on its side nose down. It's almost buried by sand now.' He looked ruefully towards the cave mouth. 'At least, I've got the kit out, but I won't be able to get the vehicle going.'

She knew then she was extremely lucky he had been driving. He'd saved her life again. Three hours later, the storm had still not abated.

Conor glanced at her somber face several times in between essential tasks and sensed what she was feeling. She hadn't said a thing about it, but he longed to tell her self-pity was destructive, that she was here now and she had to make the best of it, but he hadn't the heart. She'd taken enough flak already.

'Lie down and try to rest,' he said, 'there's nothing else we can do until the storm blows over.' But it was easier said than done. All she could do was go over what happened again and again. When Conor analyzed the crash, he concluded she must have hit her head and lost consciousness for a moment, but Lucy felt sure shock had blocked out the memory.

So, in the first hour following the accident, Lucy was good for nothing and only lay there, watching him crawling in and out of the entrance, wrapped up like a mummy, salvaging their kit, the arms, ammunition and anything else, which was valuable, from the battered Jeep.

She was still badly shaken by the crash and sat listening to the howling wind, huddled miserably on top of two sandy sleeping bags, which he made into a rough bed. Depression was kicking in now and, gloomily, she analyzed the decision she'd made to come along.

She was beginning to believe she'd probably been wrong in making it. Her only consolation was it had been made for the right reasons. At that moment, Matt seemed very far away indeed. Lucy also begun to realize her presence was fast becoming more of a hindrance than a help.

She heard Conor swearing when he found the sophisticated radio wouldn't work properly. She couldn't take in what he was saying when he tried to contact Khalid, because he'd set it up as near as he dared to the cave entrance.

Finally, he came over, brushed the dirt and dust from his face and body and sat down to explain to her, 'I've tried to get through to Khalid, but I don't know if I succeeded. Dust and sand storms interfere with radio transmissions. All we can do at the moment is pray the storm stops.'

He was hoping Khalid had received their position but, privately, he wasn't sure if the message got through. It was like history repeating itself, a mirror image of the chopper crash, but he certainly wasn't going to let Lucy know he'd failed.

'But how long will it last?' she asked hopelessly, staring at the cave entrance, where the sand swirled mercilessly and the wind blew great heaps of it inside.

'Hours maybe. We just have to sit it out. There's nothing we can do.'

145

'It's so frustrating,' she retorted.

'I know, but try not to worry about it. Now I'm dying for a drink.' They ate some more of their rations, finished off the melons and drunk a small quantity of brackish water. Then he sat back on his elbows, looked at her steadily and said surprisingly, 'I wish we'd met in England instead of here.' She turned on her back and lay, looking up at the dim, dark roof of the cave.

'Do you?' she asked, wondering what brought on the confession. She'd been hoping for the last month to learn the truth about him and, now, after all the trauma they'd experienced, it suddenly happened.

'Yes, I do.' He knew he had to do something to cheer her up. To make himself feel better. Suddenly, it seemed a good way to spend the time. 'Come on. Tell me a bit more about yourself, your job. Where you work, for instance. What's your office like?'

She grimaced, although she seemed to perk up a little then. 'There's not much to tell,' she replied. 'SOAS is a modern building. Concrete and glass. I'm on the first floor near the Admin rooms. It isn't a real office anyway. I share it with Kim. She's a postgraduate researcher in Sanskrit. I translate things for her sometimes, manuscripts, for instance. Otherwise, I'm out and about a lot.'

Suddenly the life she'd enjoyed in London seemed extremely attractive. How many times she'd said she hated the place, when things went wrong, when she was under stress but, at that moment, she would have given anything to be back there.

'Don't worry,' he said. 'I know how you're feeling. Would you be surprised if I told you I get homesick sometimes, too?' She was regarding him doubtfully.

'Yes, I would.' she replied candidly. 'You don't spend a lot of time in England, do you?'

'Well, I'm not at my desk a lot.' The lie had been unconvincing anyway. 'But it doesn't mean I like traveling all the time.'

'You don't have to play games with me,' she said. 'Come on, own up to it. When were you last in Whitehall?' He considered the question.

'A few months ago, when I was being briefed on your case. I'm not playing games. Although I've been around a bit,' She still looked extremely skeptical. 'I still consider England my home, you know.' He stared in front of him glumly. 'I get sick of all this sand too. As well as the job.'

'Then why do you do it?' The question was cruelly direct.

'It's been my life. I haven't known much else. That's the truth.' After school, there was university. Then the Leila tragedy struck. Afterwards, he'd gone into the Paratroopers and then he'd been drawn into the thick of the problems in the Gulf .

'So it's been all war, war, war then?' Maybe

she was reading his mind? He ignored the sarcastic edge in her voice.

'Not exactly. I admit I've seen a few scraps in my time and found myself in some unpleasant hot spots.' He stopped talking and she watched him take off the camouflaged flak jacket. She wasn't surprised to see he was wearing a shoulder holster, complete with pistol.

'Well, I guess I don't have to hide this any more,' he said, taking off the holster, pulling out the pistol and laying it down carefully beside the sleeping bags. Her eyes stared at the weapon, then probed his face. Her look was disconcerting, making him feel fairly uncomfortable. 'Just in case someone surprises us,' he said. She shivered involuntarily. He went on,

'At least I get sent off on some worthwhile missions these days. Like rescuing your brother, for instance.'

'And you believe we'll succeed?'

'I hope so.' Suddenly, her blue eyes were strafing him indignantly.

'I hate all this subterfuge,' she said. 'Why couldn't you just tell me in the beginning you were Special Forces instead of pretending to be some hot-shot civil servant?'

'You know I couldn't. It would have been impossible. Anyway, you've found out now what a monster I am.' His eyes narrowed. 'I have to keep my mouth shut. So have you.

Even though it gets to be a way of life, believe me, sometimes it's very hard.'

Then, suddenly, he was crouching down beside her on the sleeping bags . . . She lay there quietly for a few moments, her mind searching for a reason she felt his nearness so acutely when, in truth, she ought to have despised him for all his evasions. Next moment, she broke that awkward silence with a rush of words.

'Everything is so horrible now, the storm and the crash. What we've been through over the last few days. I'm sorry, but I can't help going over it,' she sniffed, feeling tears stinging her eyes. She curled herself up sideways in the fetal position, facing him.

How things suddenly began to happen between them, she didn't know, but it seemed just a natural progression after all they'd been through. It was as if she and Conor had been transported from their own world and its harsh realities into a different time and place, where they were simply a man and a woman thrown together by chance and who were madly attracted to each other.

As if each were tuned into the other's wavelength and when the dialogue ceased, feelings stronger than either of them could handle began to take over.

'I understand what you're feeling,' he replied sympathetically, lying down beside her then, turning his lean body towards hers, he

149

leaned his head on his elbow and looked down at her protectively. 'It's all right. It's all over now.' To his utter surprise, he could see she was sobbing quietly.

Next moment she raised her head and stared at him from frightened eyes, 'You know what I'm really afraid of. That all this will be for nothing. Maybe Matt is dead and coming with you has been a terrible mistake. I'm holding you back. Without me tagging along, he might have had a chance.'

Anything Conor could have said in response would only have been to confirm the fact, and would have surely made things worse.

Instead, he shifted his position and stretched out beside her, laid his arm loosely around her neck and awkwardly stroked her curls. Although the light touch was meant to soothe her, it did just the opposite, making Lucy's fraught nerves zing, while outside, the gale was still howling as it played every devilish game it knew at the mouth of the cave.

'I hate that noise,' she said.

'Don't worry. It can't hurt you,' he replied softly. 'You should think of it, like I do.'

'How do you?' she asked, turning her face up to his. 'Please tell me. I want to know.'

'Well,' he said gently, 'I've been in the Middle East a long time now and they believe out here, that the noise of the wind howling is nothing to be afraid of. In fact . . .' he smiled, as he tenderly brushed a wayward strand of hair out of her eyes, 'the legend goes that the sound it makes is the spirits calling . . .'

Lucy shuddered and he must have felt it too because he put out his other arm and slipped it quietly around her waist and held her close to him. Although he promised himself nothing must happen between the two of them, he could feel himself falling into the old trap. Now he didn't care.

'They're not evil spirits,' he murmured, almost to himself, 'only the souls of those whom we loved in life, walking on the wind. Staying with us all the way. Our loved ones . . . like your dad, for instance.' But he didn't want to think about Leila's spirit. He wanted to hold on to this girl, so he could forget.

Lucy listened to his words breathlessly, hardly able to believe what was happening between them. He was not doing or saying anything, except holding her to him quietly. What was he thinking about? Did he want to go any further? Was he just trying to comfort her?

Lucy shivered as she re-lived the whole horror of the incident, but she still felt she couldn't break into his secret silence. Then she felt his arms tighten about her. 'You're still suffering from shock,' he whispered gently in her ear. 'Try not to think about what happened' She shivered again.

Then his hand began to slowly caress her back, rubbing it quietly, gently as if she was something precious. Lucy was overcome by a feeling of well-being, far removed from anything she ever felt before. It seemed right they were there together. Right what they were going to do.

'I'm trying not to think about it,' she murmured, 'but it was so awful. When you told me to move and I thought I couldn't.' She snuggled into him.

'But you could.' She nodded in response. 'You were only winded,' he comforted. 'I think you were unconscious for just a few seconds.'

'Maybe.' She thought about when she tried to move after the crash and how it hurt. It still did, but not too much.

Then she put out her hand, stilled his and brought it to lie upon her stomach, just under her breasts. 'It still hurts just here.'

'That's where I fell on top of you when the Jeep crashed. When it hit the rocks.' He realized then sense had finally deserted him. His willing hand explored her waist, then strayed upwards to those beautiful breasts, which he wanted to touch so desperately, but hadn't been able to tell her how much. His mind was emptying itself of anything but her. He was smiling as he heard her gasp with surprise at what his fingers were doing.

He was holding her tightly now and the feeling of her body molded into his was wonderful. He knew it was up to him how far he wanted to go. He realized she wasn't going

152

to stop him. He could feel it in every bone of his body was aching for her.

He thought of how she had just lain there after the crash and how he'd been crazy with worry. Even when he asked her to move, she'd remained motionless.

In reality, he'd been out of his head because he thought she was dead. He'd hated himself then. For not stopping her going with him, for making a balls-up of everything again. He had very nearly killed her. He'd had no option, but to drive as fast as he could. It had been a matter of life and death. He'd been so bloody grateful she was still alive. He wanted to soothe her now, do beautiful things to her. To make up for how he'd treated her.

Lucy's heart was beating so fast she felt she could hardly breathe as his hands gently explored her body. She felt the heat of him through her thin clothes and she knew instinctively this was what she wanted for a long time.

The next moment, neither of them felt the hard rocky floor beneath as he rolled over and moved on top of her, stared lovingly into those beautiful, warm eyes, that were so different now from how they looked two hours ago. Then they'd been stuck together with sand, and her face tear-streaked and weary.

Conor's mission seemed very far away as he began to unbutton his shirt. He had only one thing on his mind. Her. He didn't care about anything that moment, except being close to her. He wanted to feel her naked skin next to his, to run his hands all over her body, to make love to her. He threw off his shirt and began quickly to help her take hers off too.

Lucy found herself trembling as his mouth sought her lips. Those hard hands which pulled her to safety three times already were drawing themselves down over her body and she was trembling with utter delight. Her head was light as she threw it back, her eyes closed as he explored her body with his lips.

'Conor,' she whispered, kissing his naked shoulder. Her whole body was aching intolerably for him. She threw back her head in ecstasy, clung round his neck, opened her eyes in sheer delight—and screamed, 'Conor, look out! Look out!'

The sinister shrouded figure, which towered above them silently, suddenly lunged forward like a lithe, big cat. A split second later, Conor's training kicked in. He threw himself off Lucy and dove for his gun.

Chapter Seven

The stranger scooped up the pistol first. Lucy screamed again as Conor launched at his adversary's legs and bore him down onto the rocky floor. Simultaneously, the man let go of the pistol, tore the scarf from his face and shouted wildly in Arabic. Suddenly the two men fell apart and were facing each other across the floor. The next moments were forever frozen in Lucy's consciousness.

Dazed, she watched everything as if it was in slow motion. Then, to her utter amazement and horror, she heard Conor's angry yell as he struggled to his feet.

'Khalid! For Christ's sake, man, what the hell are you doing here?'

Khalid. A terrible feeling of total embarrassment flooded over Lucy's body. She should have been relieved the sinister intruder was the guide whom she wanted to meet for so long. She could still hardly believe it. She looked up, trying to imagine what Conor was really thinking. She could hardly hear his voice over the howling of the wind. Was he feeling as embarrassed as she was? All she could do was stare dazedly at them both in utter shock.

'What were you doing creeping up on me like that?' Conor demanded, snarling, 'I could have killed you.'

155

He held out his hand and pulled the older man up. Afterwards, he started to look for his discarded shirt.

The Arab returned her stare with glittering eyes and she was suddenly conscious they fixed themselves on her half-clothed body. She grabbed at the sleeping bag desperately and pulled it further around her to hide her naked breasts.

Realizing Lucy's predicament, a contrite Conor, buttoning up his shirt and donning the holster and the pistol he wrested from Khalid, gestured to the guide to follow him.

Next moment, the two of them were standing, looking at the heap of armaments and kit retrieved from the wrecked Jeep, thus giving Lucy a chance to get dressed. After Conor explained what had happened, the men sat down on the floor by the radio, which was a good distance from Lucy. By then, she had retrieved her shirt, turned her back on them and was dressing silently.

'Seriously what did you think you were doing not warning us?' hissed Conor, but, inside, he knew he was in the wrong. What would he have done himself given the circumstances? Gone out into a raging sand storm again when he saw what was going on? Or sat down and waited for them to finish their lovemaking?

No, Khalid had done the right thing. He walked over to them to announce his presence and, given what Khalid knew about Conor's training, he went for the Glock before Conor got there first.

He had to admit to himself though, Khalid could not have expected to catch him in flagrante delicto.

Khalid held his eyes steadily and answered his question in Arabic, 'Perhaps you should have told me in your radio transmission you and Miss Page were lovers?' It was Khalid's ironic way of reprimanding him. He couldn't whisper because of the wind howling.

'Keep your voice down. Miss Page understands everything we say,' Conor warned. He knew their guide was not a man to beat about the bush and, like most Arabs, he tended to be unbelievably prudish.

The Arab's eyes flicked towards Lucy, who was sitting right at the other end of the cave now, looking exceedingly angry and embarrassed.

'All the better, Kendall. I am rusty in English,' replied Khalid suavely. 'I beg your forgiveness for the intrusion but I, too, was aware of the location of these caves and made for them as soon as I received your radio transmission. I had no inkling as to what you were up to.'

'Okay,' growled Conor, 'you've made your point. By the look of you, you could do with some rest.'

'I have been walking for some time,' replied

Khalid.

'Bloody bad luck about the storm,' grunted Conor, who could see Khalid did not intend to explain as to why he hadn't shown up on the first day. 'But you made it and that's what matters. The sooner we can start off the better I'll like it but, as we can't, I suggest we all get some sleep.' The Arab's eyebrows lifted in the direction of Lucy.

'I'd like to apologize for my untimely arrival first. Don't you think you ought to introduce me?' Conor glanced over at Lucy and bit his lip at the Arab's sarcastic tone.

'Okay,' he replied lightly. 'Come on over. I'm sure Miss Page will be relieved to talk to you.' It was the last thing he wanted Khalid should find them on the point of making love.

Professionally, it was the worst thing that could have happened. It would definitely indicate to Khalid that Conor didn't have his full mind on the mission, that he had been caught unawares, that it illustrated he wasn't up to the job as, if for instance, the stranger hadn't been Khalid but one of Abdul's hired assassins, probably neither he nor Lucy would have escaped being taken hostage or even survived.

As he walked across, he knew his behavior, as a soldier entrusted with such a sensitive mission, had been entirely unforgivable.

Emotionally, he'd broken the promise he had made to himself, that he wouldn't get involved with Lucy Page even though he was attracted to her. The fact was he had and, even worse, at the moment things were about to happen between them, both had been cheated by the Arab's untimely arrival on the scene. That was bad enough but that it was Khalid, who found them together, was even more awkward, given Conor's past.

As Khalid strode behind him, Conor was extremely sorry he had put Lucy in such a position. He was also very angry with himself for not being able to control his emotions regarding her, knowing, professionally, as her protector, he had been completely out of order.

'Lucy? How are you feeling? I'd like you to meet Khalid.'

'Miss Page?' Khalid bowed his head slightly, looking down into Lucy's sun-burnt face with black, unfathomable eyes. 'So, at last, I have the honor of meeting the daughter of a famous father, who was a very good friend to the people of the Yemen.'

As Khalid extended his hand, he decided, if he had been interested in her as a woman, she would have not have been to his tastes as she was far too slim. He was not Western man. Besides, thought Khalid, I am getting too old for such thoughts. I will be granted enough beautiful women in Paradise. If he had been a youth, it might have been different. Yet, even then he had not been brainwashed like young

Northern European males into thinking that only a girl, slim as a boy, could bring the greatest sexual pleasure. They had not partaken of the ripeness of a voluptuous woman's full, soft, yielding frame which was like a precious fig to be opened by only a husband.

Yet she had the silky skin, which was highly prized by the males of his race. He had already seen her naked. Her small, firm breasts, white and smooth as a forbidden fruit, were still showing beneath her garments.

He noted too the dirty, crumpled clothes she was wearing were those of a woman of his race. Evidently, traveling swathed in Muslim robes, had not managed to constrain this young woman under the precepts of his religion, nor prevented her becoming the lover of Conor Kendall.

Lucy breathed in deeply, realizing she was being closely scrutinized by this tall, haughty man with the large hooked nose and glittering expressive eyes. There was nothing she could do, but brazen it out. She felt extraordinarily uncomfortable facing him. The old self-possessed Lucy would have found shame an alien feeling.

'Thank you,' she forced herself to reply. She was extremely angry the guide had discovered her and Conor making love. 'I'm glad to meet you at last. Conor has told me a lot about you.' The Arab lifted his eyebrows and stared at

Conor, who looked exceedingly uncomfortable.

'Has he?' Khalid replied, his fine lips twisting into a smile. 'I hope he has given me an excellent character.'

'Yes, he has, but I prefer to make up my own mind about people,' Lucy replied tersely. At that moment, she was not only feeling very angry, but her body, which had been cheated of its lovemaking, was strung up so tensely she could hardly bear it.

'Then I must defend myself to you, Miss Page?' replied Khalid.

'I don't think you need to do that,' she replied sharply. Try as she might to be civil, the Arab's suave opening sentence, regarding her father, resurrected a particular memory from her childhood of her mother's disapproving voice. When Lucy was naughty, she'd always scolded her by saying, 'What would Daddy think about you letting him down like this?'

In short, Lucy's whole self was one tangle of knotted emotions as she realized the tensions of these last fraught weeks in the Middle East were finally telling on her.

'I'm sorry the Yemen has proved to be such an inhospitable place, Miss Page.' Khalid's dark eyes lingered on her body.

'It would have taken more than a sand storm to keep me from rescuing my brother,' she said.

'Lucy is very determined,' said Conor. 'And not easily frightened. We've had one or two close shaves since we started off. Like the chopper going down.' He glanced sharply at Khalid.

'Yes, that was most unfortunate,' replied Khalid smoothly. 'And, afterwards, the Jeep turning over. Perhaps we should take heed of God's Will.'

'I don't think it was God's Will, Khalid,' was the dry reply. 'More like engine failure and a strong head wind. I'll go and get you a drink.' He wasn't going to mention how Lucy fell into the gully.

'Then I'll join Miss Page and we can chat like the English do over tea,' replied Khalid in a friendly manner.

'I've forgotten what tea is like,' remarked Lucy, hoping something would divert his attention from her. She wasn't at all keen on the way he was staring at her. He probably thought she was easy prey, but she had only herself to blame.

'Then we must make do with water,' Khalid said, sitting down uncomfortably near to her and running his fingers through his iron-grey hair, which was full of red sand.

'Here. We've enough to spare you some,' said Conor, joining them and handing his one-time friend a cup of water from his own flask. Lucy looked up at him with relief.

'Thank you. It will suffice until the storm

abates, and then I can show you where to find a new supply.' Khalid drank thirstily and wiped his mouth with the back of his hand.

'I need to rest,' he added, yawning and stretching out, while observing the glances that passed between them. Neither of them looked too happy and he couldn't blame them. After all, if he had been in the same position, he would have resented a witness to his lovemaking.

But Khalid was satisfied by his timely intrusion, saving Conor from making the worst of mistakes. The Englishman had done that before, to his cost, which resulted in the loss of two women as dear to Khalid, as this Lucy evidently was to Conor.

Past pleasures, to Khalid long forgotten, flooded fresh into his mind. The stern religious principles he adhered to, decreed this girl should be full of shame and regret at her behaviour, but he realized, most probably, she was not.

'Before you go to sleep, have you any news of my brother?' she asked. Suddenly and agonizingly, she pictured Matt being forced up a twisting goat track to Abdul's eyrie, which was dramatically thrust on top of one of those great black mountains that, now, were so tantalizingly near.

Khalid shook his head. 'I'm sorry. I have none.' The light went out of Lucy's eyes and was replaced by glittering tears, as she stared soberly in front of her.

Although the suave intelligent Arab regarded Western culture as a dinosaur, he understood tears. In his country, women kept on crying, but it was still of no use. Men ruled. Their word was law in spite of a slowly-growing women's movement, mainly run by the rich and privileged.

His close observation of this woman revealed she was very beautiful and the thought of how she had been making love a few moments ago, set him thinking about Nadine. Although his wife died years ago, he missed her still.

'You have been very brave, Miss Page,' he said. 'And courage always brings its own reward. Allalu akbar.' He closed his eyes. Nadine was sacrificed for politics as well. It had been easy to take new wives, but the first and dearest was ever in his heart. The mother of his son. He sighed at the thought of what happened to him, and Leila.

'I don't think I'm brave at all,' Lucy replied truthfully. Khalid had just informed her she should trust in God's greatness. She wished she could but, at that moment, with the storm without raging as strongly as it did within, she would have given anything to be back home.

Then Conor sat down beside them. She knew he couldn't say much in front of Khalid, but she wished desperately he would say something, even if it was only to ask if she was all right. He stayed silent. Her anxiety began to make her feel claustrophobic.

Khalid shifted beside her. 'You should lie down and rest, Miss Page,' he said. 'As soon as the storm is over, we must be off.' But she remained sitting. She hardly heard what he said. Suddenly, she felt panic rising.

Although she didn't answer, Khalid thought he would like to think well of her, if he could put aside his revulsion at her sexual failings. The girl had much to commend her. He recognized the hostile look, blazing in the eyes of this young British woman when she saw him first, as the sign of a fighting spirit, which his Nadine possessed also.

Lucy Page had dared to demand her rights from her government as his wife from her religion but, unlike Nadine, the English girl also dared to demand other rights, which should only be claimed in marriage.

Khalid decided finally he must not think badly of Lucy Page because she was sexually weak. In fact, he concluded she must have been very strong, succeeding to ensnare a man like Kendall.

Suddenly, he felt utterly weary. He needed to rest if they were to succeed in their negotiations with Abdul, whose mind he knew intimately. It had been a great source of sadness to Khalid that Abdul turned out badly. Hopefully, the present leader of their tribe might see some sense and release Matthew

Page, as long as Kendall was able to produce the right offer from his government.

However, he mused sadly, there was a possibility things might turn out much the same for the English girl as they had for Nadine. He decided he hoped the end result would be a happier one. To lose another precious spirit would be a very great loss indeed.

What he had been told about the girl before he discovered her in such a compromising position, must not color his earlier view of her, which was she ought to be held in great respect for sticking to her resolve and persuading the British Foreign Office to allow her to accompany Kendall on his dangerous mission to rescue her brother from Abdul.

As a trained philosopher it amused him to question whether her courage matched her beauty. She was young and, evidently could behave very foolishly. He had just witnessed the evidence of that.

He also wondered whimsically whether the girl thought God was on her side, and if she would be as enthusiastic to rescue her sibling, if she knew what they all might have to face over the next twenty-four hour period.

Evidently, Kendall was not almighty either, although he acted like it, when he insinuated Khalid had been in the wrong to surprise them.

If, for instance, Khalid had been Abdul,

166

accompanied by his accomplices, Kendall, as well as his girl friend, would have paid with his life for his mistakes. Kendall was not a man, who took any chances. He was always well prepared. It had been most remiss behavior in a fighting man who should have known better . . .

Suddenly Lucy scrambled up and walked off. Khalid didn't bother to watch where she was going, but he guessed she and Kendall had unfinished business. The fact was confirmed when he felt Conor get up quickly and follow her too.

You must have a hold on him, Miss Page, thought Khalid, smiling imperceptibly, if he is ready to sacrifice his career and even his life for you. He wondered if the girl realized Kendall's reputation. He decided probably not.

If the man managed to kccp quiet to her about the dangers they were facing so far, he would not be able to do so for much longer.

However, one thing Khalid was quite sure of was neither he nor Lucy Page were in possession of the real orders given to Kendall by his superiors. Which was rather unfortunate for Khalid personally and meant he needed to keep his diplomatic options open.

Sleep started to overtake Khalid, just as he was deciding there must be even more to Lucy than he first surmised if she was able to make Kendall change his life-long habits.

*   *   *

'Where do you think you're going?' Conor hissed, grabbing hold of Lucy's arm as she fumbled to put on her headdress and goggles at the mouth of the cave, which was a whirling blur of dusky sand.

'I'm going outside,' she replied stubbornly, turning her head away from him and trying to carry on with the task. Her fingers were trembling so much she couldn't even put on the glasses.

Tears of anger and frustration were already rolling down her cheeks. The thick atmosphere inside was suffocating her. She needed fresh air. She made her mind up she must get away from both of them.

'You're not going out,' he repeated, holding her back. Panic-stricken, she tried to drag herself free of his restraining hands.

'Leave me alone,' she cried. 'I have to be by myself. I can't stay here.'

'Have you gone mad?' His attempts to restrain her were becoming more serious. They were struggling now. 'You can't go out there. You'll get lost.'

'I don't care!' she shouted back. 'I'll sit under the Jeep.'

'Oh, no, you won't. And you do care. I'm not going to let you go. If you want to kill yourself, then do it somewhere else. Not when

168

I'm responsible for you.' He was extremely angry then, especially because he knew whatever was happening to her was his fault, but he could see she was determined to go outside.

He found himself having to drag her away from the entrance. She continued to resist, but she was tiring as her slight build was no match for his strength. As he found himself succeeding at last, she began to sob, 'Conor. Stop, please stop. Let me get out.' She was panting hysterically. 'I don't want to be in the cave any more. I can't bear it.'

He glanced across to see Khalid stirring. There was no way the Arab was going to be witness to this farce. He thought quickly. 'Okay, Lucy, anything you want. I'll help you, if you don't want to be with us.'

Then he felt her go limp with relief, which gave him the opportunity to slip his arm firmly round her waist, so she couldn't run off. There seemed no chance of that now, because she felt like a rag doll, leaning against him for support.

'That's good,' he soothed. 'Just calm down. There's another small cave that leads off this one. You can stay in there, but I have to come too.'

He didn't mention the vermin, which might be lurking in the depths. There was no way he would let her go in there alone.

Supporting her with one arm, he pulled the

torch out of his belt and switched it on. Then the two of them moved slowly and painfully forward.

A few moments later, Lucy ceased sobbing and straightened a little as he illuminated the neighbouring cave with his torch.

'Feeling better now?' he asked as they went further inside the cavern, where the roar of the wind, reverberating against the ancient stone, was only a muffled roar, like distant thunder.

The air inside felt cooler and clearer, reviving Lucy. Soon, several sweeps from Conor's powerful torch revealed there were no unwelcome neighbours like snakes or scorpions, hiding in the shadows. Then, suddenly, she pulled away from his protecting arm and slid down gratefully onto the floor.

'Right,' he said, breathing heavily from the exertion of dragging and pushing her. 'What's all this about then?' Holding the torch away from her eyes, he squatted calmly beside her, until his own got used to the dimness and he switched off the torch to conserve the battery. 'Come on, now. Tell me. Why are you so upset?'

He waited awkwardly, wanting to comfort her, but not knowing how. He felt it was best he kept his distance from now on. His calm matter-of-fact voice wrought the opposite effect, making her even more frustrated.

She looked up at him quickly, then buried her head in her hands again. In reality, she was trying to control herself. She had conquered those sudden and horrible moments of hysteria, which plagued her before and, now, she could feel anger replacing the fear and bubbling over.

She hadn't expected him to say anything in front of Khalid. Why wasn't he saying it now? Why hadn't he ventured some sympathy instead of trying to browbeat her? Didn't he know how awful she felt when Khalid appeared? How she'd agonized about what happened between them? But, maybe he was used to making love to every girl, who was foolish enough to be taken in by his charm. Maybe it didn't matter to him? In fact, maybe nothing mattered.

As Lucy wound herself up, all the good resolutions about keeping her temper and doing everything Conor said, flew out of the cave, like sand in the face of the wind. She decided he was no better than any of the men she'd known, almost as bad as her old boyfriend, Nick, who let her down umpteen times. Now, he had the nerve to pretend he didn't know why she was so upset.

'Come on now,' he repeated, 'what's this all about, Lucy? You were perfectly all right a few moments ago when you were talking to Khalid.'

He suddenly realized he'd said the wrong thing because a moment later, Lucy was facing him, her eyes blazing with indignation. 'No, I was not. I was not all right. How could you think I was?'

'Okay, hold on,' he said, surprised at the force of her reaction. 'I realized you were a bit tensed-up.'

'Tensed-up? Is that what you call it?' she cried. 'I'd say it was more than that, wouldn't you?'

'I grant it was an awkward situation, but it didn't really matter.' He was trying to placate her and failing miserably. 'I'm sure Khalid understood.'

'Yes, I'm sure he did,' she retorted sarcastically. 'Just what did he understand? That you and I were having sex?'

'Not sex.'

'I know that. Besides, I think it did matter.' She delivered the line like a bullet hitting the bull's eye.

'Well, of course it mattered. I don't mean it didn't.' He was tangling himself in knots.

'Well, why did you say it didn't then?' she challenged.

'What I meant was it didn't matter because it won't happen again. It was very wrong of me.' He meant it with all his heart.

'Was it? And it won't happen again,' she repeated, her eyes flashing fire. If she'd been in her right mind and not felt so mad, Lucy would have laughed outright at his pathetic efforts at subterfuge.

'No, it won't, I promise. It was

172

unforgivable.'

'Right. That's it then. Now we know where we stand.'

'Do we?' He was puzzled.

'Yes. Now, if you don't mind, I'm going back in there. I can tell you, I'm keeping as far away from you as possible.'

'Lucy! Hold on,' he said frantically, switching on the torch as she jumped up. 'What's the matter? What have I said?'

'It's what you haven't said,' she snarled. 'Now please leave me alone. I don't want to talk to you any more. Ever.'

'All right,' he called. Catching up with her, he found himself bristling at her high-handed attitude. Did she think it hadn't hurt him too, leaving off like that?

He couldn't understand what was going on in her head. It was natural enough her being upset by what he'd done, but to say she wasn't speaking to him any more was a bit rich. 'You don't have to be like that,' he said, detaining her.

'Oh, but I do, I really do,' she snapped, shaking his hand off her arm. 'And I don't want to talk about what happened any more.'

'Suits me,' he retorted, relieved. At least, they'd got it off their chests now and, in his case, he was feeling better. At least, they understood each other. There was no way he would try and get close to Lucy Page again.

He watched her stalk across the cave and

roughly pull out one of the sleeping bags from underneath a snoring Khalid, who groaned when she did. Next, she dragged it as far away from the Arab as she could and lay down, face turned away from both of them.

He felt a pang at that moment. It was a pity she had such a short fuse but, then, he remembered her eyes, which seemed even lovelier when she was in a temper. It made him want to make her tell him she was sorry. Then he could tell her too.

As Conor stared up into the darkness, he found the idea excited him a lot. He felt that old familiar stirring inside as he remembered what it was like holding Lucy's body close to his. Every moment they'd shared came flooding back and overwhelmed him. If Khalid hadn't been there, maybe he would have gone over to where she was lying and tried to make up with her.

He sighed. He decided he wasn't surprised Lucy Page didn't want to have anything more to do with him. He'd had his chances and let her down all the way.

He closed his eyes wearily and turned over again and again. For the next few minutes, he shifted about uncomfortably as he attempted to sleep and shut her out of his consciousness. He convinced himself if he'd tried, she would probably have sent him packing. It was quite clear she wasn't interested in him any more.

However, as he drifted off, inside his head a

tiny voice insisted to Conor that maybe, just maybe, things might have been very different between the two of them if Khalid hadn't turned up and put his big foot in the middle of it all.

Lucy never felt so alone as she did then. She was more than tired, but she couldn't sleep. She questioned herself over and over again as to why the hell she was in such a state. She concluded it was because she was lying in a cave in the middle of a desert, with two men only a few feet away, who were about as sensitive to her needs as two blocks of wood.

When she first met Conor, she never suspected she would have been foolish enough to allow him to get near to her. She should have kept well away from him.

But, as time went on, she had been drawn to the idea he was a different man from the arrogant, overbearing civil servant, who met her at Sana'a airport. Now, he seemed to have reverted to type. Why couldn't he have told her he was sorry for what happened? As a woman, she needed sympathizing with. She felt herself wallowing in self-pity.

If only he'd been sensitive enough to say something to make her feel better. Instead they rowed about it.

Finally, Lucy concluded it must be because he considered her nothing more than a one-night stand. She couldn't bear it.

She prayed silently for the storm to stop so

175

the three of them could get on with what they set out to do. She promised herself from then on, she was going to concentrate on rescuing her brother, who meant more to her than any other man in the world.

How she longed to see Matt again. His face rose up in front of hers. He was wearing that attractive smile, with which he teased and ensnared all her girl friends. She wondered if Matt had ever been in the position she was now. Maybe she would never know? Perhaps they would never have the chance to talk to each other again?

The pull of home was so strong in her then, it made her stomach churn. Then she told herself being homesick would do Matt no good, only make her good for nothing. She needed to pull herself together. She would bring her brother home, even if she was forced to plead with Abdul for his life.

Lucy remembered the day she set off for the Yemen. Her mother finally dried her eyes and pulled herself together enough to say, 'I wish you wouldn't go, darling. I blame the Foreign Office for allowing you to. Losing Matt is bad enough, but to think you might be next is even worse.'

She remembered her words, 'But they said I'll be able to help Mr Kendall. I know about the true nature and background of Matt's project and he doesn't.' How naïve she'd been. She found out to her cost Conor didn't need her at all

'I don't want you to go,' her mother sobbed. 'Your father was always off somewhere and look what happened to him. I married an adventurer and gave birth to two children, who are just as bad. You're too like him. Stubborn as hell and far too intelligent for your own good.'

But Lucy took no notice of anything her mother said. What would have been her reaction if she could have seen her now? As Lucy lay on the cold stone floor of the cave, she tortured herself wondering whether it would have been better if she had.

She shivered as she tossed and turned, thinking of that wearisome, long, frightening silence after Matt was kidnapped. Now, the silence around her was still filled with bitter pain. If only things had turned out differently, if only Khalid hadn't surprised them.

In spite of how she was feeling about Conor then, a brief tantalizing throb ran through her as she remembered how it felt being with him, how he held her tight and soothed her fears. She knew that was what she needed now, but it was too late.

As she listened to the muffled roaring of the gale, she remembered what he told her about the ghosts, who walk on the wind. Maybe the spirit, she loved most, was still around and knew what she was going through.

She closed her eyes. 'Are you there, Daddy?'

she murmured. 'If you are, please keep Matt safe. Please let Conor . . .' But, next moment, Lucy forgot what she was going to say and drifted into sleep.

Chapter Eight

Later that afternoon, Lucy woke into an eerie, silent world. She didn't even notice the gale had dropped because, as she opened her eyes and stretched, she realized she had been woken by someone shaking her shoulder roughly.

'Come on. Wake up. You need to hear this,' Conor growled. He indicated Khalid, who was squatting, staring intently at a map spread out in front of him.

'Okay. Give me a chance,' Lucy snapped indignantly, trying to make sense of what was happening. She'd never been very good first thing. Then she realized he had woken her up, her head was aching and it wasn't morning after all.

'What time is it?' she blinked, unable to focus on her watch.

'About five in the evening. You've been asleep for three hours. Come on.' There was no reference to what had happened between them. It was as if he had forgotten it completely.

A few moments later, wrapped in the sandy sleeping bag, she flopped down awkwardly beside Khalid. To her annoyance, the Arab looked alert, while her eyes, swollen from sobbing, felt as if they were doused in pepper.

As the Arab regarded her coolly, she could have ripped his precious map into shreds. No doubt he was comparing her sluggishness, with his apparently superior freshness. What upset her more was Conor's attitude.

He'd settled himself on the other side of Khalid, wrapping his arms round his long legs. He didn't even look her way as he sat there, just ignored her completely throughout the conversation.

His silence and detached demeanor could only suggest to Lucy a complete lack of interest as to her welfare. She was sure if he'd spoken out loud, his opener would have been, For God's sake, get on with it, before I'm treated to further histrionics from the girl.

Fuming, she decided his attitude was unbearable. How could he totally ignore her presence, when they had been so close just a few hours ago? Suddenly, the memory of those few, wonderful moments when they were lying together wrapped in a tender embrace, overcame her, bringing instant tears to her eyes.

Bravely, she forced them back, her hot irritability dissipating into cold, dull misery. Lucy felt empty inside, his utter disregard for her feelings twisting like a knife in her chest. How could he ignore her like that?

She felt even more anxious as Khalid began his technical explanations. She knew she wasn't taking anything in properly. Allowing herself to be upset by Conor was distracting her from concentrating on a plan that might save not only her own life but her brother's.

She hated herself for allowing her emotions to affect her common sense, which told her feeling so miserable only made a bad situation worse. Her stupid self pity was compounding all her earlier anxieties, about Conor judging her presence as superfluous and her input as totally unprofessional.

However, he hadn't much to say to Khalid either, only interspersed the guide's words with several curt suggestions, which the Arab agreed with, or did not take on board.

But, occasionally, Conor's dark eyes swivelled towards Lucy. Instead of showing sympathy, they seemed to be reminding her Khalid was the leader now and to keep her mouth shut. She felt he was warning her to listen to the Arab, and take notice, to obey Khalid just as she promised she would him.

So she kept quiet, realizing she was quite evidently number three in the pecking order. Obviously, her opinion was of little worth to either of them.

But, in spite of her hostile feelings towards him, she couldn't blame Conor as much as she blamed herself.

Ten minutes later as Khalid finished outlining his plan for the journey she was still full of self-pity. She concluded her bad temper was not surprising, given her sleep had been broken constantly by all the upset, as well as the noise of the wind.

'Right,' said Conor tersely, turning to Lucy. 'Got all that? You'd better get dressed,' he ordered. 'Put on all your woolens, and the cap.' She knew better than to question why. Next moment, he added the reason, 'It'll be freezing when we set out.'

But, as the two men stood up and shook the sand off their clothes, then started to talk rapidly between them, she realized the silence excluding her from them, was proving to be just as cruel as the howling gale.

*   *   *

Half an hour later, Lucy, who had gone past caring how she looked, was standing at the cave entrance, dressed in black combat gear and trying to remember the details of Khalid's explanation. He'd said they needed to set out as soon as it was dark. She shuddered at the thought as she stared across the landscape.

As far as the eye could see, the wind's devastation was apparent. Its merciless breath had driven across the narrow ribbon of the plateau, which led to the foot of the nearest peak, and blown it into a bleak moonscape of great sand castles, which lay basking silently in the tawny rays of the setting sun.

How could anyone ever cross those valleys and mountains of sand in the dark? Lucy stared miserably upwards to where the great orb of the sun floated in the air, ready to sink behind the sharp, jagged peaks, where Matt lay hidden. It was an unpleasant glory.

Behind it, she imagined the darkness, hovering like some sinister bird, waiting to swoop down and gobble them up in one swift mouthful, dragging them deep into another black desert night.

She shivered apprehensively as Conor and Khalid made their final preparations for the assault on Abdul's mountain Eyre. The men were now packing up the kit bags, and covering over the half-buried Jeep.

Snatches of what Khalid said flashed through her mind. Suddenly her stomach began to churn alarmingly. She'd been waiting so long for the moment to come but, now, it was almost here, she felt a thousand times less brave than when she set out full of high hopes to rescue Matt.

Her eyes swivelled to a still taciturn Conor as he checked and re-checked the equipment? Did he feel anything like she did at that moment? Suddenly, she wished she knew. She would have given anything to have asked his opinion and to have been reassured everything

182

would turn out all right.

Then she remembered how she'd told him she never wanted to speak to him again.

Suddenly, Lucy was ashamed of her hysterical outburst. Now, it was too late and he had evidently taken her hasty words to heart. The last hour proved he'd washed his hands of her.

And Khalid seemed to be in charge now. Watching the men working closely together, gave her the opportunity to observe their reactions to each other. After only a few minutes, she'd already decided as far as she could make out, the relationship between them was a strange one, a mixture of comradeship and unease.

The mundane conversation, which started inside the mouth of the cave, about what was the best thing to do with the machine gun before they reached Abdul's camp, now progressed into something more significant. She could see they'd walked away from her on purpose, that they didn't want her to hear.

But she felt a duty to herself to find out every tiny thing she could about their past. Khalid was very evidently part of Conor's.

Since the moment the Arab surprised their lovemaking in the cave and she noted Conor's reaction to his arrival, she convinced herself learning everything about her two companions was an exercise, linked to her own survival.

So, moving quietly, she slowly eased herself

183

out of the cave and along its outer rocky wall, until she was within earshot. Then she positioned herself behind a large boulder. She decided, if they noticed her, she would wave at them. Then they would assume she was there for her personal needs. Which in one way was true.

Lucy didn't like eavesdropping but her intuition was still telling her she needed to hear everything that was being said. Breathlessly, she watched and listened as they stood staring at the huge heap of sand, surrounding the Jeep.

'That storm really buggered things up, didn't it?' Conor's lips were set in a hard, thin line.

'In more than one case,' retorted the Arab calmly smiling.

'I'm not in the mood for innuendoes,' snarled Conor irritably, glancing at his watch. Lucy's face flushed, knowing what he meant. 'If the weather had held, we would have been able to hide this old crate in a convenient spot and use it as a getaway vehicle if need be. That was the plan anyway.'

'What is done, is done,' replied Khalid philosophically.

'God's Will again, eh, Khalid?'

'Why not? At least, you can't blame me for the storm, Kendall.'

'So what can I blame you for, Khalid?' Lucy strained her ears, trying to catch every word.

She could see by Conor's expression he thought the Arab was hiding something.

'I had nothing to do with your crash.'

'In the helicopter?'

'Come, Kendall. Did you think I meant the Jeep?' The Arab smiled suavely. 'Now why would I want you and Miss Page to crash? We're old friends, and she is a lovely girl.' His amused eyes lingered on Conor's face. Lucy was incensed at what she felt was needless sarcasm. 'Besides, we're here to do a job. We depend on each other.'

'Maybe.' Lucy could hear the doubt in Conor's voice. She felt sudden anxiety. If there was no trust between them, how could they present a united front to Abdul. Did he really think Khalid had something to do with their helicopter crashing? It made her feel sick.

Conor went on, 'Let's suppose the situation suddenly changed and you were no longer in favour of us making a deal with Abdul. Whatever has happened in the past, whatever you think about what he's doing now, he's still your . . .'

To Lucy's utter annoyance, Conor turned his head. She craned her neck desperately so she could hear the rest of the vital sentence, but it was lost. However, Khalid's voice was raised indignantly now.

'That is not fair, Kendall. I have my country's welfare at heart. Our relationship is irrelevant. What Abdul is doing at present is

185

very bad for all of us. What good has snatching the Englishman done for the Yemen? Once more, we will be labelled by your people as kidnappers and murderers.'

'Matthew Page has only himself to blame. He's a young idiot, who should have known better than to mess around near that shrine.' Lucy bristled at his denigration of her brother's character.

'The desecration of the shrine was only an excuse concocted by Abdul. You, of all people, should know that,' retorted Khalid. Lucy stiffened. 'Many evil deeds have been committed here in the name of religion.'

'Do you think the Yemen has an exclusive on that kind of thing, Khalid? Remember I spent a few years in Northern Ireland with one of those across my knees.' Conor indicated the machine gun.

'Just so. Both you and Abdul were too young to personally experience the struggle our people undertook to bring unity to the Yemen and what we lost by it.'

'Ancient history.' Conor snarled, turning his back on Khalid and squatting over the kit bags.

Lucy waited apprehensively, wondering what was coming next. Her heart sank. What hope was there to get Matt out, when the two men she was depending on solely were so evidently at odds?

'Such history must not repeated, Kendall.' The Arab's tone was placatory now as he

186

walked over to him. Conor straightened and looked up at Khalid. Lucy had seen that expression before. She knew he was regretting what he'd just said.

'You're thinking of Nadine?'

'Yes. I can see by your face you're remembering Leila.' Lucy swallowed as she saw Conor scoop up a handful of sand and, quietly, let it trickle through his fingers. He was nodding.

'Nadine was very brave. It was not your fault she and Leila died in that way, Khalid.'

'Nor was it yours, remember. I have never held it against you.' With a pang, Lucy saw Conor's expression change to utter gloominess. Evidently the girl they had just mentioned must have been very close to him.

'But you must agree both deaths were the inevitable result of the struggle for freedom,' Khalid continued. 'Slavery can be of different kinds. My wife believed that implicitly.'

He put out his hand and touched Conor's sleeve, then withdrew his hand. The other was staring into the distance, his face set. Khalid added, 'Don't be so hard on yourself, Kendall? You must learn to forgive yourself.'

'I can never do that,' was the surprising answer. 'I let them die.' His fists were clenched by his sides.

'Be careful, Kendall,' warned Khalid. 'A man must learn to forgive himself, or he will

187

be eaten up by bitterness.' He put a hand to his own breast. 'Look, Kendall. I am still sad but, as you said, what happened was not my fault. My wife tugs at my heart every day, but I know she held nothing against me. That I'm not a lost soul.'

'Spare me the sympathy, Khalid. I was damned from the day she and Leila died.' A sharp pang stabbed Lucy. What had he done to make him so bitter?

'And Allah is merciful. Come. We have been through too much, you and I. We should be able to trust each other.'

'Did I say I didn't trust you?' Lucy was shocked by the misery of Conor's expression. Whatever happened in the past had left its terrible mark. It was then she was desperate to know who Leila was and her ensuing fate and, even more important, if Conor was truly to blame.

'You did not say so, but I saw it in your eyes when you were talking about your helicopter,' replied the guide.

'You're an old fox, Khalid, and an old soldier. You know where men on opposing sides would be if they always trusted each other implicitly.' Conor smiled briefly and Lucy could see he had regained control of his emotions and the tension was lessening between them.

'Just so, Kendall. Then we must stick together, wherever our loyalties lie.' As they

188

continued to talk, Lucy pressed herself back behind the rock, where she concealed herself. Could it be true Conor and Khalid were enemies and once on opposing sides?

Once again, her suspicions as to Conor's real orders came rushing back. When he came clean and divulged he was not a civil servant but a member of the Special Forces, she had been afraid there were other things he hadn't told her.

Now she was sure. Where did that leave her? In the same boat as those two poor women, whom they were just discussing? What happened to them? Conor said Nadine had been Khalid's wife. So was Leila Conor's wife? It was a sobering thought.

She bit her lip. Khalid said Conor needed to forgive himself. Could she trust him any more? She wanted to desperately, but he was keeping too many secrets from her.

Was he really interested in getting Matt out? How he spoke about her brother showed he blamed Matt for being kidnapped. Perhaps he blamed her for everything that was happening to them. If he did, then there was not much chance he would see to it they got back safely.

For a moment, Lucy felt very scared indeed, then she started to pull herself together. She wasn't going to take things lying down. She was going to fight as she always did. He was taking her for a fool and she didn't like it.

Setting her lips in a stubborn line, she thrust back her hair from her face and stepped out from behind the rock. She decided, whatever happened, she was going to have it out with Conor and make him tell her the truth.

'Hi,' she said, as the men swung round. 'How's it going?'

'Not bad. Why?' asked Conor brusquely. Lucy felt uncomfortable as she saw the expression on his face. She found it almost an impossibility to hide anything from him before and she felt instinctively he guessed what she was thinking.

'Only asking,' she replied lightly. 'I suppose I'm anxious to be off.'

'I think we all are.' Khalid nodded. 'Miss Page is to be commended for her eagerness, don't you think, Kendall?' Conor didn't reply but his eyes strafed Lucy's face.

'It's quite easy to explain,' she retorted. 'I can't wait to see my brother again.' The men exchanged glances.

'Then I suggest you let us get on with this, or you never will,' stated Conor bluntly. Lucy's face flared at the obvious snub. 'You still look burnt. I should make the most of the shade while you have the chance.' He indicated the cave. 'Get back in. The last thing you—and we need—' he flicked a glance at Khalid, 'is for you to go down with heat stroke. We've enough on our plates.'

'You don't say,' remarked Lucy sarcastically.

'Don't worry. I will.' With that parting shot, she stormed off into the cave. Conor glanced at Khalid again and shrugged. To his annoyance, the Arab was smiling sardonically. A moment later, Conor strode off after Lucy.

She swung round as she heard his footsteps come up behind her.

'What the hell did you think you were doing ordering me about like that?' she hissed. Her eyes took in his set expression. He was really rattled and for one tiny moment, she was scared she had gone too far.

He glared at her, his heart thumping as he saw her lovely pointed breasts rising and falling. Once again, he thought how beautiful she looked when she was angry. He was spoiling for a fight. For anything, that allowed him to be near to this tantalizing, infuriating girl. Next moment, he grabbed hold of her arm. 'Let me go,' she cried. His hard fingers were pressing uncomfortably against her bone. 'How dare you order me about,' she repeated.

'You are one stubborn, little . . .' he bit back the word. He could see she was trying to goad him. 'You promised you'd behave yourself. Remember?'

'I didn't know what I was doing then.'

'What do you mean?'

'I mean then I didn't know what you were capable of.' She was panting as she tried to pry herself free. 'You think you're God, don't you? And I know nothing. Well, I do.'

191

'What are you on about? What have I done?' He stared at her blankly.

'You know very well what you've done. I know you want to get rid of me. Well, you won't. I'm here to stay,' she shouted.

'I think you should shut up,' he retorted, 'Khalid might hear.'

'And that wouldn't do, would it? Not after last time. I don't care what he thinks about me.' She shook her head, making her damp curls tumble wildly round her face. 'Do you know how you've humiliated me? How you've made me feel? Do you understand? Now let me go.'

'Okay.' His grip relaxed. It was doing her no good, getting worked up like this. He realized she was talking about Khalid finding them together. She mustn't have meant what she said to him earlier on, that she wanted nothing to do with him any more. Perhaps he ought to take her in his arms? Was that how to calm her down? He grinned involuntarily, thinking it would do the opposite for him.

'First you . . .' she struggled for the right words, 'you try and make love to me, then—'

'Try?' The word jarred him into defending himself. She wasn't making any sense. 'I would have said you were up for it.' Her eyes flashed dangerously.

'Don't insult me,' she retorted. 'I only wish we'd—'

'What?' he breathed. Next moment, he took

192

her in his arms and was pulling her taut body close to his. 'You wish we'd carried on, don't you? So do I.'

Her body froze as he pressed his hard mouth against hers. She was ready to struggle free but all she was conscious of was a burning desire for him rising inside her. It was like a fire raging in her very soul.

She felt the strength drain out of her body and her whole self melt into one useless mass, as Conor's lips opened hers, drawing the sense out of her head, awaking her starved emotions. Her mind went totally blank for one long, delicious minute as she abandoned herself to his embrace.

As he felt her body relax, he would have given anything in the world to carry on, but he couldn't allow himself to. He'd been caught out once and he couldn't afford to be so careless again. He needed his strength to get them through what was coming.

He cursed himself silently for not being able to resist her. It took all his years of training to force himself to let her go, because getting too close to Lucy Page could be fatal for them all.

She gasped at his abrupt withdrawal. 'See,' he said softly, 'Neither of us needed to try, did we?' A second later, Lucy lashed out, but he caught her hand in an iron grip.

'What's up?' he frowned. He couldn't make her out at all. First she wanted him, then she was ready to knock the hell out of him.

'How dare you kiss me like that,' she seethed. He held on to her calmly as she struggled.

'I don't know what's up with you,' he repeated, 'blowing hot and cold. Still . . .' he relaxed his grip, 'have it your own way, you stubborn little fool.' He watched her as she chafed her wrists, sorry he'd hurt her. 'You can keep on pretending you can't stand me if you want. I can't fathom the reason, but it won't do you any good. If we get out of this, I'll make you understand . . .' He stopped, afraid of what he was about to say. He wasn't ready to declare himself yet.

'And if we do,' she spat, 'you'll never make me do anything. Nor ever kiss me again like that.'

'Want to bet,' he challenged coolly. He'd never understood women and she was worse than most. She was scrubbing her mouth with a dirty hand, as if she wanted to get rid of his taste. He knew better after the way she'd kissed him back. He added, 'Whatever you think of me now, you'll do what I say and not interfere. You're here to take orders and not to give them. Understand!'

'You arrogant bastard,' she gasped.

'I know what I am,' he smiled. 'That's why I'm still alive.'

'But Leila isn't.' The words shot like a bullet straight to his heart.

'What did you say?' Lucy stood her ground

as he towered over her. 'How the hell do you know that?' His face was pale under his tan.

'I know, because I heard you and Khalid talking. Who was she, Conor? What did you do to her?' Lucy could see she had regained control.

'That's enough,' he snarled.

'Am I going to end up like her?' She knew she'd gone too far then. Next moment, he was gripping both her shoulders. As he glared into her face, his dark eyes flashed angrily.

'Whatever you think you heard, you've nothing to do with her. You're not the least like her in any way. Do you hear? Don't ever mention her name again.'

Lucy saw with a shock there were tears glittering on his lashes and, suddenly, she was ashamed of what she'd said. Of how she'd hurt him.

'I won't,' she said, bringing her lips together stubbornly.

The atmosphere in the gloomy cave fairly bristled with tension as they faced each other in a stand-off. Then, suddenly, they were plunged into utter darkness as the dying sun finally slid behind the mountains.

She heard him fling away from her and out of the cave. 'Oh!' gasped Lucy. She stood shocked and motionless, waiting for her eyes to get used to the dark.

As the dim outline of the cave's mouth started to appear, all she could think of was what just happened between them. She began to grope her way towards the entrance, where a torch beam was already flickering.

One of them was coming to help her. Would it be Conor? She knew how she'd hurt him, but he'd hurt her too.

'Okay, I'm here.' The beam caught her full in the face and chest, then swivelled onto the floor, making a white circle of light.

As he led her out silently, she was half-sorry they hadn't made up, but still angry about the way she'd been treated.

'Are you okay?' he asked. His voice wasn't rough any more.

'I'm all right,' she replied, following him. Her head was full of what happened between them.

A moment later, she was standing in between Conor and Khalid, the white torch light illuminating their boots. 'We have to keep it down,' Conor said, 'or we'll be seen for miles. Here. Put these on.' She'd never imagined she'd ever wear night-vision glasses She looked up into the men's faces, which were illuminated by a red glow.

'Better?' She nodded. The three of them huddled together. Khalid's features looked extremely sinister, close to hers.

'Listen to me carefully, Kendall. As for you, Miss Page. I've no desire to pry into your personal affairs.' Lucy glanced quickly at Conor, but his lips were set in a hard line, and

196

he fixed his eyes on Khalid. 'But I am warning you, any animosity between you must be put aside.' At that point, Conor gave a funny little grunt. 'We work together from now on as a team.' continued the Arab. 'I lead, you follow.'

Lucy jumped as she felt strong hands on her belt. Next moment, a rope was clipped on. 'Just in case, Miss Page. The paths are treacherous. You will be following Kendall. If you cannot keep up, pull hard on the rope. Try, please. You have nothing to carry. We will take it all. We must make the outskirts of the village before dawn.'

Then the men were shouldering their heavy kit bags. Lucy nodded, trying to get used to the glimmering, red, desert world she could see through her glasses. Five minutes later, they were ready. Khalid turned and hissed. 'Remember, we are a team.' Next moment, they were off.

*   *   *

Throughout their struggle along the stony mountain tracks, Lucy strode onwards bravely, almost mechanically, determined not to let the men down. Whatever happened, she needed to keep up. The pace they were going, was not too bad and, at least, she could see where she was headed, although looking at the world through infra-red was like being in a dream.

But her concentration continued to be punctuated by the best and the worst moments from the past few weeks. After they'd struggled over endless sand dunes and, finally, hit level ground beneath the mountain, they rested for a few minutes. 'It's all up from now on,' Conor said as he handed her a water bottle. 'But you're doing okay. Drink, then take this.'

'What is it?' she asked, looking apprehensively at the tablet.

'Salt. It'll restore your water balance. Put it in your mouth and swallow it.' She obeyed. 'Then we're off again.' He stood up and went over to Khalid, who was consulting the compass. Soon, they were on their way again, this time climbing upwards tortuously, their boots slipping and sliding on the shale.

Once or twice, she skidded back down terrifyingly, and was hauled up again by the men. It was then she realized how lucky she was to be roped to Conor. She was given plenty of time to think as they ascended the mountain paths.

She remembered how many times he'd saved her life already and, suddenly thought she understood their relationship was founded on something far deeper than she'd imagined. The importance of trust in the face of danger. Everything else at that time, including emotional ties, shouldn't matter.

But, in spite of her total dependence on him

and her admiration for what he could do physically, she could see that was not enough. Inside, she knew, as a woman, she needed more.

Whether there could ever be as strong an emotional link between them as there was a physical one that night, was a question she couldn't answer. This wasn't the time to ask it.

As they made their assault on the mountain, she was being tested to her utmost but, the next time they rested her head was still full of what passed between them.

She and Conor had been thrown together in difficult, even alien circumstances. She'd been available and, also, totally dependent on him in every way. The important question she needed to ask herself and him was, had he taken advantage of his superiority? She told herself she just didn't know. She was totally confused as to their real relationship.

What she did know was how she felt. What her emotions were telling her all along. She really cared about Conor. Khalid said they should put their differences aside and behave as a team; and she was trying to desperately.

She concluded she must try something else as well. To conceal her feelings for him. Besides, and although she didn't want anything to take her mind off the mission, she couldn't help thinking of the last time he'd kissed her. Had it shown she meant very little to him? Or he couldn't resist her?

199

She risked a surreptitious look at him as he crouched, head resting on his arms, folded across his knees. What made him tick? She was no nearer to finding that out then when she studied his back in the helicopter.

He was a hell of complexities. At that moment, she couldn't pigeonhole him, nor make him into something he was not. What he had done for her over the last few weeks was to save her life. What more could he do? Why should she expect anything else from him? Maybe he couldn't give any more?

Sudden misery overtook her as she thought of how she'd taunted him about the past and how he'd flung angrily away from her in the dark cave. She didn't know how she could ever apologize to him for mentioning Leila because, then, he might find out what was really behind the way she, herself, behaved.

Lucy understood very well in spite of how she'd screamed at him, what she'd called him and how he'd reacted, she truly cared about him.

Oh, Conor, she said to herself, biting her lip. What do you want from me? Are you still in love with her even though she's dead? One day, you're going to have to explain.

Then, next moment, Lucy felt herself struggling to her feet as Conor started up, peered at his watch and flung his arm out in a beckoning gesture, which meant they were on their way again.

Chapter Nine

The first light of dawn was beginning to streak the sky with slashes of carmine as an exhausted Lucy and her two companions made their dash from the protection of an outcrop of sharp rocks and scrambled into a shallow hole, which had been scoured out of the rock by ages of winnowing winds.

They lay there, breathless, for a moment, then Khalid roused himself and crawled up the rough rock side. 'Look, Kendall. Across there,' he whispered, turning. Conor joined him.

'What is it?' Lucy asked, too weary to move. How many times had she imagined herself back home in her cozy bed? What would she have given to snuggle into her pillow now instead of having a sharp rock pressing into her backbone? She shifted position and nearly cried out loud in pain.

'The village. It's in sight,' Conor said, taking off the night glasses and putting them away. He gestured to hers. 'You don't need them now. The sun will be full up soon.'

She wanted to ask what was going to be their next move, but she resisted the impulse, knowing they would tell her in their own good time. She was learning. Then Conor was beckoning her. She crawled over wearily and handed him the glasses.

'Are you all right?' he asked, putting them into his kit bag.

'I think so,' she answered, 'but I'd like to take my boots off.' She stared at her feet, which felt terribly sore.

'Well, you can't. Not yet,' he replied curtly. Their relationship had almost reverted to what it was when they'd first set out in the chopper. He instructed. She obeyed. He was turning to Khalid now. 'This is a good place to hide the weapons and the radio.'

'That's why I brought you here,' replied Khalid. Lucy lifted her eyebrows. Not the slightest gesture escaped the guide. He was staring at her now, his eyes glittering in his blacked-up face. 'You've done well, Miss Page. Let's hope it lasts.'

'It will,' she replied grimly, not daring to think about how she was going to move, but she couldn't give up now. Her legs felt like boards and she was sure her feet were covered in blisters. Everywhere on her body hurt. She forced herself not to think about stepping into a warm bath.

She shook the idea out of her head and began to move her limbs gingerly. She felt if she didn't, she would seize up.

But, at least, she'd made it. She hadn't finished herself off by sliding down a crevasse or plunging from a precipice. They should both be grateful for that. Her death would have caused them too much trouble.

'What are you thinking?' Conor asked suddenly.

'That everything hurts,' she grimaced.

'I know,' he replied, 'but you made it.'

'Can I look over the top as well?'

'I'll give you a hand,' was the surprising reply, 'but keep your head down. They've probably spotted us by now and there might be snipers around.'

'Of course,' she replied, thinking how glad she was she was still wearing the bullet proof vest. Then she felt him grabbing her hand.

'Up you come,' he said, pulling her, 'now take a peep.' As she cautiously inched her head over, she squinted up to the dawn sky dizzily, to where, high above them, a bird of prey was hovering.

'A buzzard,' he whispered. 'There are loads of them up here. They love floating in the air, looking for their breakfast.'

Lucy could see they were right on top of a mountain, holed-up on a rectangular plateau about a quarter of a mile wide. The view was breath-taking all around them and, in the distance, at the far end of the plateau she could make out a cluster of houses, clinging dizzily to a rocky outcrop. Exactly like those villages, she looked down on, during her first ride in the ill-fated chopper.

'Did we climb all the way up here?' she murmured, dreamily. She could hardly believe it.

'Yes, surprisingly.'

'Wow,' she said, an amazed look on her face.

Conor smiled at her reaction. She didn't know it was the kind of smile he reserved for his lads, when they'd done a good job but, suddenly, she was grinning back at him, her teeth showing stark white against her blacked-up face, her eyes shining under her bedraggled, curly head, which was crowned with the black woollen cap.

As he looked at her triumphant expression, Conor was thinking that as crazy woman as she could be, she'd managed to accomplish a man's job with a hell of a lot of courage.

'Hopefully, that's where they're holding your brother,' he explained. He felt she deserved the explanation.

Lucy could scarcely breathe at the thought of seeing Matt again but, at the same time, hardly bear the thought he might be dead. She didn't want to think about it, but she needed to face it.

'How do you know?' she asked, hoping her voice wasn't trembling like she was.

'Because it is my village,' interrupted Khalid, 'and where Abdul hides out. Wherever he is, your brother will be. Now, we will hide the gun. Then you make contact on the radio.'

'Right,' Conor nodded. Next moment, he was crouching down and tuning in to the base camp. Lucy's heart thumped on unmercifully, as she listened to him giving and receiving terse commands and wondered how long it would be now before they met Abdul. Then Conor switched off.

'Well, they know where to pick us up now.' Lucy picked up Khalid's sharp glance as he said it but Conor didn't take any notice as he turned to her. 'When we do get out in the open, Lucy, you must do exactly as I tell you,' he warned.

'I will,' she promised.

A few minutes after they'd hidden the machine gun and their pistols, Lucy watched Conor take out and unfold an identical silver sheet to the one he'd used earlier to attract Colonel Ali's helicopter. That rescue seemed years ago now. He spread it carefully out in the hole. Afterwards, he pegged it down. He glanced up at her. 'Another necessary precaution just in case radio communication gets difficult. As long as we get back to this hole in one piece, they'll be able to pinpoint the spot and pick us up.' It was a comforting thought.

Soon, Lucy found herself walking between the two men down the track towards the village, with Khalid preceding them slightly, holding a white flag high which Conor produced from his kit bag. She realized then how right he'd been about being prepared properly. If he hadn't been so circumspect, they would have been stranded by now.

But, she could see, by the way his eyes darted around warily, he must have been as nervous as she was. It was then they saw several black dots, like ants, appearing from the village buildings, their silhouettes outlined against the red sky. Then more, and more.

'They know we're here,' hissed Conor to Lucy. 'Remember do as I tell you.' Minutes later, the trio were face to face with a small band of bearded men in black robes coming slowly down the goat track, pointing rifles in their direction.

'Here they come,' said Conor, bracing himself. Lucy felt her mouth grow dry as they approached. Having never been in such a menacing situation before, she breathed in deeply, ready to face whatever might happen.

After all, she told herself, this is what I came for. It won't be long now before I see Matt again. She knew she must continue believing that. It was then she felt a comforting hand on her arm. 'Don't worry,' said Conor softly, 'they want what we've got, as much as you want your brother back.'

She didn't ask him what he meant, just prayed he was right. Then one of the men broke out of the group and started to run towards them. She felt Conor stiffen, but he stood his ground.

Next moment, to her utter amazement,

Khalid threw the flag down onto the ground and the two Arabs embraced. 'He has come back! Allah be praised!' shouted the grey-haired tribesman exultantly, as the others came up.

'Keep calm,' whispered Conor. Next moment and, for the first time in her life, Lucy found herself staring down a gun barrel while, by her side, Conor was already being frisked.

She watched the Arab search all his pockets thoroughly, withdraw everything and scrutinize every object carefully. Anything the man thought was of use to him was placed in his own robes, and the rest returned to Conor.

Then it was her turn to face the humiliating experience. She submitted with closed eyes and slowly stiffening body, as she felt their hands all over her. It was a very frightening experience.

The men drew back. They did not search Khalid, who opened his arms in an expansive gesture. 'Are you satisfied now we are carrying no arms?' The men nodded. 'Good.'

He indicated Conor and Lucy. 'This is Miss Page.' She nodded briefly, full of revulsion, as they stared at her with dark, glittering eyes. 'And Conor Kendall, who has been sent by the British Government. I brought them here. Now, take me to Abdul.'

*   *   *

Lucy looked round the bare room with walls and floor made out of stone, where she and Conor had been forced to wait for hours while Khalid went off to meet the terrorist leader.

The whole place smelled of cow dung which, when dried and mixed with sand, formed a lining for the walls. Into two of the outer walls were cut a couple of small barred windows. Surprisingly, the shutters had been thrown wide open, which meant at least a slight breeze was doing its best to alleviate the stifling heat of the midday sun.

Conor had not spoken very much, since they were shown into the room by an old woman wearing traditional Arab dress and flipflops on her feet. The floor was covered in a piece of tatty linoleum and there was an unlit oil lamp in the corner, which the woman picked up and carried away. 'Just in case we try to set the place on fire,' he muttered, by way of an explanation.

Later on, she'd returned bringing them a bowl of chapattis mixed with milk to eat, and a pitcher of water. After the old woman left and she'd heard the key grate in the lock, it crossed Lucy's mind, they were prisoners too, but she wasn't going to voice her fears.

In spite of its horrible look, the food hadn't tasted too bad, while the brackish water, which they poured into the bowl and took turns to drink, was almost as good as wine to two people, who were so desperately thirsty.

When they'd finished drinking, Conor wiped his mouth on the back of his hand. Later, Lucy found herself remembering every minute detail, and especially the incident that followed.

She'd sat back on the narrow metal bed, which was the only furniture in the room. All it possessed was a dirty-looking blanket for a counterpane and a small heap of cushions for pillows. It evidently doubled as a settee.

Instead of sitting beside her, Conor suddenly squatted down on the floor and began to unlace her boots. She could hardly breathe as she felt his strong fingers untie the laces and loosen the tongues.

'What are you doing?' she asked.

'Well, you said your feet were killing you.' His eyes twinkled with sudden amusement. Then, carefully, he'd pulled off both boots and to her utmost amazement and pleasure, took off her socks and chafed her feet gently back to life.

'I'm afraid you've got blisters,' he said softly, as he examined her heels, 'but it's only to be expected, after all that hard walking. Usually, you have to harden off your feet for a hike like that. Just a minute.' Then he was slipping a hand into his jacket pocket and withdrawing a tube. 'Luckily, the bastards didn't take this,' he stated, flipping open the cap.

'What is it?'

'Wait and see.' Next moment, he was applying the cream to her blisters. She sighed with pleasure, wanting him to go on for ever.

'Thank you,' she said gratefully, her eyes fixed on his head as he bent over her. She felt a mad impulse to put out her hand and stroke his short hair, but she repressed the feeling.

'That's okay. You needed it,' he said, stopping after a few moments. 'Now you should put your feet up and rest them while you can.'

Next moment, he was straightening up. Then, pressing the cap back on the tube, he replaced it in his pocket. Obediently, she swung her legs on to the bed and, just before he walked over to the window, he squeezed Lucy's shoulder briefly in a gesture of encouragement. 'Chin up,' he said.

'But what about you? Aren't you tired?' she asked.

'Oh, I'm all right,' he smiled wryly. He'd been standing at the window ever since.

She glanced across at the silent figure, thinking for the hundredth time about his complexity. What did he really feel for her? Rubbing her feet earlier on, and that tiny gesture when he touched her shoulder, must have indicated he still felt something. Such things were insignificant now, given their position.

Perhaps he was looking for an escape route? She couldn't see his expression but, by the set

210

of his shoulders and his whole stance, she knew he was alert, ready and waiting for something to happen. She guessed he was making contingency plans.

Although she wished he could have shared his thoughts with her, she decided it would be better to leave him alone. Doubtless, he'd a great deal on his mind.

She didn't disturb him immediately but, eventually, she heaved her tired body up from the bed and joined him at the window and peered out to be rewarded by the sight of a dizzy drop, a space full of swooping birds of prey.

'This house is built right into the mountain face,' she gasped. She knew then any earlier thoughts she'd entertained about escaping, hadn't the slightest value. No one could climb down that precipice without ropes and, even then, it would be very easy to slip and be killed. 'I can't believe we're that high,' she said.

'Unfortunately, we are,' was his unhelpful response. Then she returned to the bed and sat down again, thinking about Matt. She looked across at the door, then up to the ceiling, feeling totally frustrated.

A few hours ago she'd been striding freely through the dark, the thought of finding and rescuing her brother uppermost in her mind, spurring her on into attempting and accomplishing unimaginable physical feats.

She'd actually scaled a mountain at night.

Now she was helpless. Where was he? Would she ever see him again? Had it all been for nothing? She felt panic rising and swallowed it down. She wanted to be reserved like Conor. She mustn't show all the fear and frustration she was feeling. It would do no good, only make things worse. She needed to keep cool.

So she passed the time by imagining Matt's whereabouts. Perhaps he was being held next door to them? The doors were so narrow that one was forced to enter them sideways. Or was he locked away upstairs? When they'd been brought in to the house, she'd seen a narrow flight of steps, which must have led to the second storey?

Maybe he was chained up? She knew what happened to hostages? How bad a state was he in? Maybe he wasn't even in the village?

Her heart ached for her brother again. She felt anxiety rising. The need to see him immediately was like a physical pain. Every time she thought about Matt and what was happening to them all, her stomach turned over alarmingly. Suddenly, she remembered what Khalid said. Where Abdul is, your brother will be.

Suddenly she found herself wishing irrationally for something to happen, anything, good or bad. She dropped her head into her hands, trying to clear her brain, forcing herself to remember why she was here and reminding herself it had been her own choice to come.

Calmer now, she raised her head and stared at Conor's broad shoulders, remembering too how she fantasized about the things he'd been through, before the chopper crashed. Now she was bang in the middle of the same kind of situation. Inside, she knew if anyone could get them out, he could.

Suddenly, as if he was reading her mind, he turned from the window and came over to sit down beside her. His very presence was giving her courage. She smiled faintly, and his smile was a quick flick in response.

He breathed in deeply and looked round, his eyes following hers. 'Nice wallpaper,' he murmured. 'This is probably the best house in the village.' It was his way of trying to cheer her up.

'It's certainly got the best view,' he added. 'I'll bet not many of the other poor sods, who live round here, are so lucky.' He smiled grimly.

'I hate the smell,' she said, wrinkling her nose, forcing back the tears, which threatened to burst out and spill over. She sniffed, remarking, 'I wonder if all the rooms are like this.' It was just something to say.

'Try not to worry.' He seemed to be reading her mind. His sympathetic words made her want to cry even more.

'But . . .' she hesitated, almost afraid to ask

him again 'but how do we know Matt's still alive?' She saw he was considering her words carefully. Just like he'd done when they had been on very good terms. Suddenly, she would have given anything to have gone back to that time before he and she were carried away by their emotions.

In fact, what could have been so wonderful, spoiled everything. She wondered if he felt the same as she looked into his eyes.

'Come on, Lucy,' he encouraged. 'Don't give up now. We made it here and, honestly, I don't think your brother's dead.' She was staring at him, hanging on his every word. He had to give her some hope.

'Don't you?'

'No. I think Abdul has more use for him alive.' It was true. The terrorist would hang on to his hostage until the bitter end. Conor knew Abdul would be banking on not handing Matt Page over until he got what he wanted. That was the way the whole thing worked. By bargaining.

He regarded Lucy's worried face and cursed himself for not being able to have made her stay behind. There was a probability before long, she might be held hostage too. His face set in a grim mask. Not if I can help it, he thought with new resolve.

'Why are you looking like that?' she queried, feeling her voice tremble. 'You don't think Abdul can be trusted, do you? That he'll renege on your offer, whatever it is?'

'I didn't mean to scare you, Lucy,' he replied, looking at her sideways. Then he leaned back and stared up at the ceiling, then down again. 'Unfortunately, none of us know Abdul's mind. Except perhaps Khalid.'

He wanted to tell Lucy why he and Khalid were chosen to do the job, but he couldn't. In fact, neither the Arab nor Conor even revealed the true nature of their mission to each other. The Arab had no idea Conor's orders were to make sure Abdul didn't double cross any of them ever again.

Khalid's motives for wanting to meet up with Abdul were very different. Matt Page's incarceration had been just the excuse he needed to get to the young terrorist. Otherwise, Abdul wouldn't have entertained his presence, because he hated anyone pointing out the folly of his ways, or taking advice. Especially Khalid's.

Conor was convinced Khalid was making a last-ditch attempt to bring Abdul round to his way of thinking. In the circumstances, it was natural for Khalid to want to believe that might happen and he still had some influence. Tribal affiliation was deep-seated in the social identity of the Yemen and these tribes' histories spanned two thousand years.

However, one of his fears was Khalid might have guessed his orders. If the guide had, then it was likely he and his supporters were behind the sabotage of the chopper and it would be most unlikely Conor and the Pages would make it out alive.

He shook his head at the somber thought, then realized Lucy was staring at him curiously and was about to ask more awkward questions. Suddenly, he decided he needed to explain, if only a little. At least he owed her that.

'What did you mean earlier on when you said Abdul wants what we've got?' Lucy asked.

'I meant I have some bargaining power. That my orders from the Foreign Office regarding Abdul are quite clear. It would be dangerous for you and your brother if I was to disclose them prematurely. They're for Abdul's ears alone.' He managed to hold her glance steadily. That was the truth at least.

'I didn't come all this way to fail in the end, Lucy.' He wasn't half as confident as he sounded, but keeping up team spirit was part of the job.

'Thank you,' she said. He looked at her anxious face and his heart went out to her. He would liked to have comforted her but he didn't know how.

Besides, he felt he would the last person she would look to for comfort now. The main thing was he had a job to do, and that was to get her and her brother back safe to the Army camp.

He glanced at his watch. With luck, Ali was on the move by now. He prayed the Colonel wouldn't bugger things up by being too eager. He needed the choppers to keep to their schedule.

'How long has Khalid been in there now?' she asked. Her own watch stopped working ages ago, probably because it was clogged up with sand.

'An hour or so,' he said. 'They've plenty to talk about.'

'How long has Khalid known Abdul?' He breathed in deeply and she could see, for some reason, he didn't want to answer. Biting her bottom lip, she shook her head determinedly. 'What do you think is happening between Khalid and Abdul? I can't bear any more waiting.'

He put a hand on her arm and let it lie there, noting her torn sleeve and disheveled appearance with a pang of sympathy for both her and himself.

'Don't get upset,' he replied. 'I'm not sure what's going on, but I can guess.' She was staring at him with her full lips parted, revealing her white, even teeth. He wanted to kiss her fears away.

Even after rolling about in the dust and having her clothes torn on rocks, she still had the power to excite him. If only he could pull her down on the bed and make love to her like he'd tried to do in the cave.

'Go on,' she begged. Then he squashed the ridiculous thought flat. He'd promised himself

217

there would be no more lovemaking. How could he even think about it at a time like this? He concluded he must be going mad.

'Please?' She could feel his hot eyes strafing her body. She knew she must look a terrible mess after all that scrambling about over rocks in the dark. At least, he couldn't think she was a wimp any more.

'If the rest of the village are terrorists, why isn't Khalid?' She wished he'd hurry up with the story and take her mind off where they were keeping Matt for a few moments. He didn't answer. She went on, 'I was so surprised when I saw that man embrace him, like his long-lost brother. I've never understood why he's helping us.' She was determined to get to the bottom of what she heard when she was eavesdropping. To find out whether Khalid was friend or foe.

'They're not all terrorists up here, Lucy. For example, that old lady who brought us the food.' Although what he said was true, a lot of innocent people were very likely to pay dearly for harbouring Abdul. They would be sacrificed as surely as Leila was. He grimaced. 'Most of them are ordinary peasants caught up in something they're unable to avoid.'

'Like kidnapping my brother?' Lucy's eyes glinted.

'Yes, I suppose so, but you can't tar them all with Abdul's brush.' In his time, he had seen too many lives spoiled by war. He frowned.

218

There were no grey areas in his business.

'You're speaking as though you know him.'

'I do . . . at least, I did.' He regarded her steadily.

'How? Who is he?'

'Well, believe it or not, Abdul was educated in England. He's a product of the British public school system.' She gasped. 'And I've known the family for a long time.' She was staring at him with hostile blue eyes.

'You're not going to tell me you went to school with him?' If it was meant to be a joke, it fell flat.

'Not likely. Don't worry, I'd have beaten him up.' The frown, which creased Conor's brow, relaxed.

'Well, that's something,' retorted Lucy. 'Come on, tell me, how did he turn into a terrorist?'

'It's a long story and one I can't go into now. One thing I am sure about is, his word's not to be trusted. The other side of the coin is he trusts no one either. Except perhaps Khalid.'

'Why?'

'You'll find out soon enough. Khalid is our trump card. He's probably the only one, who can make Abdul see sense. Khalid used to be the leader of the tribe and tribal loyalties run deep.'

He glanced at her quickly. She was taking it all in and, at that point, he couldn't tell her any more about the very special relationship that existed between Khalid and Abdul. She would soon find out

'He should take notice of him, given his past position,' he went on, 'and I hope he will, because Khalid, at least, can see a future for his country. Khalid's never been solely a political animal. Being a philosopher and an intellectual, he realizes kidnapping all and sundry isn't the best thing for a state, who wants to present a civilized image. I'm afraid our Abdul's a fanatic, who has difficulty in seeing no further than the end of his nose.'

He didn't elucidate by telling Lucy exactly what a murdering swine the young Yemeni was.

'Khalid certainly appears to be popular up here,' replied Lucy dryly, thinking again of his warm greeting by Abdul's men.

'There's no doubt he has some pull,' he replied. 'He's revered by the tribe. He's the local boy, who made it big a long time ago. He and his wife Nadine were part of an elite team who worked progressively with the military.' Lucy held her breath. Perhaps she was going to find out about Leila too?

'But, when the political system in the Yemen was unified in 1990, Khalid was put in charge of one of the governorates, which took the place of the tribal units, which were abolished.' Lucy nodded. She was familiar with the history behind the politics.

He continued, 'Naturally, that didn't go

down too well in some quarters and Abdul, who's a true fanatic, fell out big time with Khalid.'

'I see. Is Khalid still married?' Lucy was desperate to know how Nadine and Leila died.

He looked at her keenly, wondering what the question had to do with anything. 'No, he's a widower.'

'Did they have any children?' she persisted.

'Yes,' he replied warily, 'but what's that got to do with it?' He couldn't see where the conversation was going. Nor did he want to, in case the truth slipped out. Besides, he was growing anxious something might have happened to Khalid. If it had, then they were finished.

'Sorry, I was only asking,' retorted Lucy. 'Tell me some more.'

'There isn't a lot I can add,' he replied, 'except Khalid probably wants to heal the rift with Abdul, and he saw his chance by offering to mediate with him after the kidnapping. His behaviour has reflected badly on Khalid's tribe.'

'I see,' said Lucy thoughtfully. She looked round again. 'I feel as if we're prisoners. We aren't, are we?'

'I don't think so,' he assured her. 'Abdul will want to hear what I have to say. After all, I'm representing the British on this and you're a British subject.'

'I feel a lot better inside now,' she said, then

221

grimaced. 'But, outside. Well, I wish I could have a wash.'

'Maybe you'll get one soon, but it'll be well water that's carried up the mountain track daily by the women. They have a hard life of it.' He was thinking about Leila. How she'd toiled for that bastard of a husband. How he'd tried to save her.

'I don't know how they stand it,' remarked Lucy.

'Sometimes, they don't.'

'What do you mean?'

'I mean that some women risk their lives to get away. Especially those who have been sold into slavery.'

'Are you speaking from experience?' Lucy was beginning to guess. Had Leila been one of those unfortunate women?

'Perhaps.' She could see he didn't intend to proceed further with the conversation. She had seen that look on his face before. Total shut-down.

It was then they heard heavy footsteps outside. Conor jumped up from the bed and stood, facing the door. He turned, 'Remember, do everything I say.' Lucy nodded, her strung-up nerves sending a rush of adrenaline around her body. Next moment, the key was grating in the lock.

'Khalid,' said Conor, feeling relief rush through his body. The guide was dressed in fresh, black robes. He was accompanied by two tough-looking men, carrying guns. Behind them, the diminutive old woman was hovering.

'The time has come, Kendall,' replied Khalid. He stared at Lucy. 'You will go with the woman, Miss Page.'

'But I don't want to. I want to go with you.' Lucy looked at Conor helplessly. All of a sudden, real fear was biting into her. If they were separated, she might never see him again.

'Don't worry, Lucy,' replied Conor quickly. 'I'm sure Abdul intends to meet you later.' Khalid was nodding. 'May I have a minute with her in private?' Khalid raised his eyebrows then shrugged an assent. A moment later, Khalid and the men withdrew and pulled the door shut behind them.

'Listen,' said Conor urgently. 'You're only being sent to get cleaned up, before you see him. It's not worth antagonizing him by refusing. He's not a man to be trifled with. I'm afraid what's really behind this is a woman wouldn't be considered fit to take part in important negotiations. You'll have to grin and bear it. Remember, I'm not going anywhere. You'll be okay.'

She bit her lip fearfully. Next moment, he lifted his hand and touched her cheek then, to her utter surprise, he bent and taking her face in his hand, briefly kissed her on the lips. She closed her eyes momentarily, her heart fluttering and her mind asking a thousand questions.

A second later, that tender moment was over and she felt his protecting arms let go, leaving her empty and vulnerable. He was shaking his head. 'I'm sorry, Lucy.'

'It's all right,' she said. 'I'm not.' He stared at her blankly for a moment, then added,

'Remember, I won't leave you. Whatever happens, you have to keep cool.' Then Conor turned and banged the door with his fist. Immediately it swung open and the Arabs entered again.

Lucy didn't like the look in Khalid's eyes. It reminded her too much of when the guide surprised them in the cave.

Khalid smiled. 'I'm not depriving you of Kendall for ever, Miss Page. He and my son need to talk.' She could hardly believe what she'd just heard.

'Your son?' cried Lucy. 'Abdul is your son?' Her mind was grasping at the possibilities, trying to make sense of the knowledge. No wonder Khalid was so important. No wonder he'd been picked to lead them to the terrorist's camp. But why hadn't Conor told her?

'Conor, is it true?'

'Yes.' As he confirmed the fact, Lucy's heart plummeted. What other secrets didn't she know? She turned to Khalid. 'Is my brother safe?'

He nodded, then looked straight through her. She could see she would get no more out of him. She realized a long time ago the Arab considered her needs totally insignificant.

Seconds later, Conor was being escorted from the room by the armed men. She knew the brief glance he directed towards her as he went out, was warning her to keep her cool.

'Good luck,' she said, in spite of how she was feeling. Her spirits sank finally as she saw his back disappear through the door. Now she was on her own.

The old woman, who shuffled in behind the men, was beckoning her too, so breathing in deeply and telling herself she needed to keep going, Lucy followed her gaoler out, praying everything would turn out all right in the end.

Chapter Ten

Lucy washed as best she could in a tiny, dark room, which served as a bathroom. She remembered how she'd hated showering in the army camp, but this place was much worse and she wondered for the umpteenth time how people managed to live under such conditions.

There was a large tub of well water standing in a corner, but no soap. She did her best to wash thoroughly and, later, with her hair curling round her face in wet rings, she'd been horrified to find the lavatory was situated in the other corner of the room. It was only a hole in the floor, through which the daylight glimmered.

When she came out, she found the old woman had taken away her own clothes and laid out fresh ones for her. They were lying on a raised platform at one end of the room, which Lucy realized when she approached was meant to be a kind of settee but was constructed from hard packed sand and coated with dry cow dung. She picked the pair of black trousers from it gingerly. There was also a long dress to wear over them.

The garments looked and felt horribly hot, being made of some shiny synthetic material. Lucy had no option but to put them on. There was a long scarf folded beside them, made of some kind of nylon, which she knew was intended to cover her head and face, but she'd already made up her mind that was not going to happen. Instead, she put it round her neck.

And, all the time, she was on tenterhooks, her stomach turning over alarmingly as she kept on wondering what was happening between Conor and Abdul.

So she sat down miserably on the hard, narrow bed, identical to the one, which had been in the other room, and waited, trying to thrust all fear from her mind . . .

After what seemed an age, the door opened to reveal the same two men, who had taken Conor away. They'd evidently come for her. Staring at her in a hostile manner, they indicated she should cover her head with the scarf. Bravely, she shook her head. They glared at her, but did nothing.

Next moment, one of them was pushing her out of the door. Swallowing her nervousness, she made her way out into the narrow passage, which was dim, stiflingly hot and reverberated with the sound of what she guessed was the house's generator.

A few moments later, she was descending some stairs and found herself in a small hall, where a heap of cushions was piled in the corner in front of a sophisticated-looking computer system.

She guessed the hall was an ante-room to a more important chamber, because another two armed guards were standing each side of the narrow doorway facing her.

Her heart was thumping as she tried to prepare herself for whatever ordeal she was about to face. She was hoping desperately Conor would be inside. She badly needed his strength.

She and her two captors waited silently as one of the guards slipped inside. As the door opened, she could hear a hub of voices, raised in anger.

A few moments later, he emerged, leaving the door ajar. As the guards pushed her through, she was conscious only of the silence.

She felt the perspiration burst and break on

her forehead, but she threw her head back defiantly as she entered the dark, cavelike room.

When her eyes got used to the dusk, she realized it was lined with men, standing two-deep, leaning against the walls. Most of them were armed and stared at her with hostile eyes.

The smell was overpowering and she suddenly realized the stuffy room must have been situated right over where the cattle were kept.

Trembling a little, her gaze swivelled apprehensively towards the focal point of the room, a rectangular table at the far end. With utter relief she saw Conor who looked straight at her, his steady gaze encouraging her to keep calm.

She recognized Khalid's tall figure sitting by him and, some distance away from them, a bearded young man, dressed in spotless white, bending forward, his long-sleeved elbows resting on the table.

He was grinning at her, showing a flash of white even teeth, and he made no attempt to get up as the armed men led her over to stand in front of him. It was then she noticed the single pistol lying on the table. With her heart still racing, Lucy stood, facing Abdul.

'Miss Page' he said, 'We meet at last. I have been told so much about you.' His English accent was impeccable, but his manners did not match, because his cold, black eyes raked over her body rudely. She flinched under his gaze but, all the time, she was conscious Conor's eyes were fixed on her, willing her to be strong. Lucy breathed in deeply.

'Where is my brother?' she asked Abdul in a clear voice. The onlookers remained silent. 'Where are you holding him? Why isn't he here?' She looked round.

'I ask the questions, Miss Page,' Abdul growled. The urbane tone disappeared. 'I can see you are British. Here, in the Yemen, women know their place.' There was a dangerous edge in his voice and she saw Conor shift in his seat.

Lucy was determined not to be cowed. Now she'd begun, she was feeling braver already. It was like jumping in at the deep end and surfacing. 'I came here to find my brother, and I demand to know where he is. Let me see him, please.' Abdul's mouth twisted in a cruel leer and his hand strayed towards the pistol. Was he going to shoot her?

The she realized Conor was on his feet and, simultaneously, men all around the room were going for their rifles. Then Abdul lifted his hand. They froze. He was still toying with the pistol as he gestured to Conor.

'Well, what have you to say, Kendall?' Throughout the proceedings, Khalid remained seated, gazing impassively in front of him.

'She means no harm, Abdul,' Conor said, facing the terrorist bravely. 'Miss Page is upset.

She had a hard time of it getting here. She's been missing her brother a long time.' Then Abdul jumped up from his chair. He approached Lucy and began to walk around her very slowly, looking her over.

She didn't flinch this time, just kept her eyes on Conor, already regretting she'd so easily forgotten his advice of staying cool.

'I can see why you're defending your lover, Kendall,' Abdul quipped. She held her breath. Doubtless, he had learned about her involvement with Conor from Khalid. 'She's very beautiful, but much too outspoken. She must learn to keep her mouth shut. Or I shall shut it for her.'

Abdul was very close to Lucy now and, in that one brief moment, Lucy realized just how dangerously crazy he was.

'No need for that, Abdul,' hissed Conor.

'Then make her behave herself. You will be joining your brother soon enough, Miss Page. Now sit down!' Lucy saw Conor's eyes flick alarmingly, but he didn't speak, only indicated the chair where he'd been sitting.

She walked quickly towards it, desperate to put as much distance as she could from herself and Abdul, who continued to follow her every move.

The terrorist had also been watching the by-play between them with narrowed eyes. His next words were overtly sarcastic. 'Very touching. Now there is no seat for you at our conference table, Kendall.'

'I'll stand,' Conor retorted. As Lucy was about to collapse into the chair, Conor clutched her arm, preventing her from doing so. It was then she realized no one sat in Abdul's presence—except his father, who seemed totally wrapped in his own thoughts.

'Good.' Abdul took his chair again and Conor indicated Lucy should sit down too. The Arab's eyes swivelled towards her again, lingering on her face. 'Now, Miss Page, Kendall tells me you have come here to beg for your brother's life.' He sat back. 'So, I'm ready to listen to your plea. He's also informed me you are an expert on Yemen antiquities like your late, lamented father.' Lucy frowned, but said nothing.

'Now, be good enough to tell me, what did your brother think he was doing dishonouring a shrine, which was so important in our culture and to our religion?'

As Lucy patiently explained she thought Matt had been quite innocently excavating in that area, she realized indignantly Abdul was not listening to anything she said.

As she continued, she could see he was less than interested. Throughout her speech, he fiddled with his pistol, which made her nervous, or sniffed loudly and gazed around the room.

If anyone else had behaved like that when she was speaking, she would have let them know how angry she was in no uncertain terms, but she knew, at present, even the tiniest show of temper, verbal or non-verbal, would have not only been useless, but also highly dangerous. In Conor's words, she needed to keep cool.

When she'd finished explaining the reasons why Matt was there at that particular time, Abdul's smile was ugly. Lucy thought he was the least attractive individual she had ever met and it was a pity she was in no position to comment on the fact.

'Thank you for your information,' said Abdul. Lucy inclined her head. 'As your father's daughter, you evidently know a great deal about our country and its customs. Unfortunately, your evidence has done nothing to convince me of Dr Page's innocence. I'm sure you'll be pleased to know your brother is no longer on trial.' Her stomach turned over with relief, but it didn't last long.

'He stands condemned by his own actions,' Abdul added, his eyes glittering. 'You beg very prettily, but Dr Page must personally take the consequences for his foolish actions. However, I think his stay with us so far has chastened his ardour for exploration in the future.' A ripple of amusement ran round the room.

'What have you done to him?' cried Lucy, ready to leap out of the chair, but Conor brought his hand down hard on her shoulder, stopping her short.

'I can answer that, Lucy,' he said. 'I've seen Matt, and he's okay.' Conor's eyes were steady, warning her to keep calm. 'Shall I go on?' he asked Abdul. The terrorist nodded, his mouth twisting into a smile.

'Our negotiations have been satisfactory, Lucy. Abdul is going to release you and Matt. You'll be allowed to go soon.'

'Oh, thank God,' she cried, noticing momentarily how drawn and pale Conor's face was.

'But the price is high, Miss Page,' said Abdul suavely. 'You should be grateful to Kendall. He has offered himself as a hostage in your place.' Lucy went white.

'I can see you are moved,' added Abdul, 'but I assure you no harm will come to him, unless his government does not keep its promises.' She looked up at Conor, shaking her head.

'You can't do this for us,' she began.

'I have already. Don't worry, I'll be okay. Abdul's promised to release me when the choppers come to give him and his men safe passage out.'

'And the cash,' snarled Abdul, his voice, a rough growl.

'But how will you get back home?' Lucy asked, her voice trembling.

'That's for me to worry about.' Conor gripped her shoulder again. He turned to

Abdul. 'Now, let the girl see her brother.'

'I don't take orders from you, Kendall,' the terrorist spat. 'You're far too arrogant. Like your woman who does not cover her head in my presence.' The men around the walls muttered in agreement. Lucy bit her lip anxiously.

Abdul stood up and leaned over, hands flat down on the table. 'In fact, I've changed my mind already.' Lucy saw Conor's face harden. 'This woman is too rebellious. She reminds me of my long, departed sister. Poor Leila.'

He shot a poisonous glance at Conor. Lucy gasped as Abdul stared him out. She felt as if she was going to faint. Leila was Abdul's sister? And Conor had been responsible for her death. The horror of their situation finally hit home. Suddenly, Lucy feared they would never get out of this.

'Do you feel the same about this woman, Kendall? Are you ready to die for her?'

'Leave Leila out of this, Abdul,' snarled Conor dangerously. The room swung dizzily in front of Lucy's eyes and she gripped the table with sweating hands in order to steady herself. Their angry voices seemed to melt into a dark void but, with superhuman control, she brought herself back to reality by letting her head fall forward.

It began to clear a little as she felt Conor's strong fingers clutch her shoulder for comfort. She lifted her eyes and saw through a mist of tears Khalid was on his feet, facing his son. His tall presence seemed to dwarf the terrorist, who glared at his father angrily.

'You must not go back on your word, Abdul. It is your bond.' His voice was deep and full. Abdul regarded Khalid with crazy, rolling eyes.

'Don't order me about, old man! Did you think I would let Kendall and his lover live— the man who was responsible for my sister and my mother's death?' He was shouting now.

'That is not true. There's no excuse to shed more innocent blood, Abdul.' The two Arabs faced each other across the table, then the young terrorist grabbed the pistol and pointed it directly at Lucy and Conor. Fear ran all the way through her body, leaving its trickling footprints in her hair and her skin.

Then she thought of how he had tried so hard to make her stay behind. He knew all along what was going to happen and she'd taken no notice. She dared to glance up at him. He looked down steadily into her eyes. There wasn't the slightest hint of fear in his face. Just looking at him gave her courage.

Then, she felt him slip his hand into hers and place his other arm round her protectively. She stayed motionless, savouring his nearness but, realizing with a shock, her legs were trembling so much that she would have fallen, if he hadn't been holding her up. At least, we'll die together, was her sudden thought.

'You have given your word!' thundered Khalid. 'This girl is innocent. So is her brother. Isn't it enough you've already spilled so much innocent blood? What more do you want? You've been guaranteed safe passage as well as a fortune. You must let the girl and her brother go. Keep Kendall if you must until the helicopters come, but let them leave.'

To Lucy's absolute horror, she watched Abdul turn from them and aim the gun straight at his father. The Arab didn't flinch.

'Be frightened old man, You don't lead this tribe any more,' yelped Abdul, his face contorted with anger.

'Remember, Abdul, Allah will never forgive a son who murders his father,' replied Khalid calmly, standing his ground.

But, a second later, Abdul fired. The room sizzled with shock, then fell utterly silent as Khalid slumped, pale-faced, back into his chair, clasping his shoulder, from which the blood seeped, darkly disappearing into his black robes.

Conor let go of Lucy's hand and tried to rush forward to help, but Abdul's bodyguards restrained him. Abdul sniffed and twirled the pistol in his hand. 'Take them away. All of them. Let her see her brother.' He gestured towards his father. 'Put him with them too. He's no father of mine. He has grown soft and too much like his Western masters.'

A moment later, Lucy and Conor were

surrounded by armed men and were being herded through the door. Behind them, they sensed others lifting and carrying out the half-conscious Khalid.

They were all pushed on downwards, past the cave-like space where the cattle lived, out into the blazing sun, towards an outhouse with a flat roof and small, narrow windows. Lucy could see its back wall was carved out of the rock itself.

'I'm sorry, Conor,' panted Lucy, as they came to a halt outside the heavily-padlocked door. 'If I hadn't upset Abdul, this mightn't have happened. I shouldn't have come.'

Conor looked down at her face sympathetically. 'I don't blame you,' he said. 'I told you he couldn't be trusted. Abdul's psychotic. He's always been a murdering swine, but I can tell you one thing for sure.' He was quite confident he was right. 'He won't kill us. Anyway, not until he gets what he wants and, by then, hopefully, something might have turned up.'

Next moment, one of their captors was raising the bar and with a violent push, she and Conor found themselves in utter darkness, spread-eagled face down on the floor.

It was then Lucy gasped, realizing they were not alone. Something was moving, close to her. She went cold all over then, suddenly, she heard the harsh, cracked voice asking urgently in Arabic, 'Who are you? For God's sake, tell me. Who are you?' With enormous joy, she realized who owned it.

'Matt!' she cried. 'Matt. It's me. It's Lucy.' She struggled to her knees, and, next moment, just as her eyes accustomed themselves to the dark, her brother launched at her from the corner. He'd been cowering there in the dark, and flung his body at her, enveloping her in the tightest embrace she'd ever experienced.

A moment later, two more guards dropped a half-conscious Khalid roughly down on the stone floor, and, pulling the door behind them, padlocked it again, leaving them in the dark.

*   *   *

Some hours later, Lucy sat back wearily, her spine pressed against the hard rough wall of their prison. An exhausted and emaciated Matt talked himself out and, while they cried and commiserated together, a silent Conor spent his time ministering to the wounded Khalid, who groaned loudly many times. The afternoon slipped into moonlight and, now, she felt all in.

'Give me your scarf, please,' asked Conor. She unwound it and watched him use it to staunch the blood from the Arab's wound.

She didn't offer to help because she felt there was nothing she could do. Once again, she regretted she'd no training in first aid and felt acutely helpless leaving everything to

Conor, who was still groping about in the dark.

She thought about Matt, who was lying on the floor with her, his head on her lap. She knew he was in a bad way, mentally and physically, because he had been gabbling at her incoherently for ages. Now he seemed calmer. She looked down at him and, suddenly, he opened his eyes and lifted his head. 'I'm sorry about earlier on, Sis. It was like I'd forgotten my English.' Then he closed them again. She shuddered, thinking what he'd been through.

Little by little, Lucy's eyes grew accustomed to the dimness of the room, illuminated now only by the moonlight, which sent thin shafts of silver through the two narrow windows, reminiscent of those in a Second World War bunker. She sat wearily staring up at the beams, willing herself not to give up.

A moment later, she felt Conor slip down beside her. 'How's Khalid?' she asked. She hadn't heard him moan for a long time.

'He's unconscious now,' replied Conor. 'He's lost a lot of blood.'

'Will he die?' she asked, thinking of how Conor buried the pilot after the chopper crash. It all seemed so long ago.

'Maybe.' The reply was hardly audible. She shivered, praying he wasn't feeling like her, because he was their only hope now.

'I don't know what they've done to Matt,' she said, her voice breaking, 'but he seems to have lost all hope.' She put her hand out and stroked her brother's wet curls.

'Don't worry. He's been a hostage for a long time.' answered Conor. 'He hasn't slept properly for months. He's physically and mentally exhausted. It hasn't dawned on him yet, we're in the same boat but, hopefully, we won't be for long.' He pressed the light on his watch and noted the time. 'In a couple of hours Colonel Ali should be here.'

'And we'll get out?' asked Lucy.

'Yes,' he replied briefly. He wasn't going to tell her when and if they did, it was going to be touch and go, whether they survived. Ali's men had their orders like him. There was no way the authorities would let Abdul escape. In situations like that, hostages got seriously hurt.

But Conor was determined it wouldn't be the same for Lucy and her brother, although the boy was done in. He probably hadn't much fight left in him and he'd been kept in the outhouse for so long his legs were weak. In fact, he was the biggest liability, as there was no hope for Khalid.

'So what'll happen?' she asked.

'Hopefully, once Ali knows the cash has been handed over and he has his safe passage, he'll let us go,' he lied.

'But will he?' asked Lucy doubtfully. 'How can he be sure he won't be shot down?'

'He can't. That's where I come in. He'll be

240

taking me along.' There was no way he was going to hint he, himself, was totally expendable. He had no illusions, once Abdul was airborne, Conor or no Conor on board, they'd be shot down.

What he was afraid of was Abdul would insist on taking either Lucy or Matt with him as well as himself. Or maybe even both of them? He knew if he'd been a murdering swine like Abdul, he would have taken them along.

But, he asked himself, if that happened, what was he going to do? He'd been ordered to take out Abdul. Could he sacrifice the Pages' lives as well as his own? He was facing an agonizing no win situation at that moment.

He wished for the thousandth time Lucy had never involved herself in this mess.

'What are you thinking?' she asked. It was then she felt him move closer, and, suddenly, his hand was seeking and holding hers like it had done earlier on. She clung on desperately as their fingers entwined.

'About how we're going to escape,' he whispered. Inspiring confidence was all he could do.

'Thank you for everything,' she said, choking back the tears as her emotions overtook her sense.

'Hey, hey, what's this? We're not dead yet.' His attempt at a joke was greeted by silence, followed by an audible sniff. Still squeezing her fingers, he stroked her face with his free hand. 'You're not crying, are you?'

'I am,' she said in muffled tones.

'Well, don't. You've still got me.'

'Oh, Conor,' she burst out, breaking down. 'I'm sorry.'

'Why?' he asked tenderly. 'You only did what you thought was right. I admire you for it. In fact, I admire every silly thing you've done.' She didn't respond badly to the half-joke. So, taking his cue from her silence, he drew her close and kissed her lips tenderly. She didn't resist then either, but she didn't kiss him back.

After he released her, his heart was thumping. 'Well, you aren't yelling at me again,' he ventured.

'No.'

'I'm glad. I thought you didn't want anything else to do with me.'

'Why did you think that?' sniffed Lucy.

'You said you didn't. In the cave.'

'Oh, that. I was in a temper. It's just I-I thought you were taking advantage of me.'

'How?'

'I don't know,' she sighed. 'I suppose I thought you thought I was available and . . .'

'It never crossed my mind,' he replied.

'And what about when Khalid came in and found us? Why didn't you defend me instead of pretending it was a triviality?'

'I was just as upset as you were, Lucy, but I needed to keep up a front with Khalid.'

'You mean you were ashamed?'

'No, that's the last thing I was. I knew Khalid, being unbelievably prudish, would take it as a sign of weakness and accuse me of not having my mind on the mission, which he did. Men like Khalid are totally focused. They don't let anything or anyone get in the way of what they intend to do.'

He breathed in deeply. Confessing to Lucy was proving to be more difficult than he'd imagined. 'I used to be like that. I know it sounds callous, but it was vital to let him think what happened between us meant nothing. Even though it did. Am I making sense?' She didn't answer. 'You do believe me?'

'I'm trying to,' she replied. 'So you're saying you've changed?'

'I suppose I have, in some ways. It was very wrong of me to try and make love to you, but I couldn't help it. I got carried away. You were so lovely and I couldn't resist you. It was a new experience for me.' He realized the last sentence was ambiguous. What he was trying to tell her was it had been years since he felt anything real for any woman.

'It doesn't matter,' she said, scrubbing her eyes with her free hand. 'It's only I felt hurt when you didn't explain yourself. It's all right, I think I understand now.'

'I'm glad.' He had never been any good at

showing his feelings. He needed someone to teach him properly. He'd been hoping against hope it could be her. Now, it was probably too late, but he was going to try.

They sat in silence for a few moments and then he risked, 'Lucy, there's something I want to tell you, just in case we never get out of this. I'm sure we will, but, just in case, I really do care about you. I've liked you ever since we met.'

She stared into the dark, hardly believing what she'd heard. She remembered all the times he'd the opportunity to say so before, and all the misunderstandings between them but, now, at last, he'd declared himself, she didn't know how to respond.

How strangely ironic it was everything had suddenly come to a head, when it might be too late. Although she realized in the present circumstances there was little to be happy about, those few wonderful words lifted her spirits in a way she'd never have believed possible.

'Aren't you going to say anything?' He was frightened he'd made another blunder by telling her.

'I'm not sure what to say,' she replied truthfully. 'I feel a lot for you as well but, because of everything that's happened, is happening now, I can't get my head round it. It's sad we got off on the wrong foot in the beginning. We've wasted so much time. If we'd met somewhere else, everything would have been so much easier.' Suddenly, her mind was pushing present horrors away, imagining meeting him in some little restaurant, sitting in the candlelight, eating and laughing together.

'You mean you might have liked me more if it had been another time and another place,' he murmured. He wasn't surprised at her reaction. He hadn't expected much, given his behaviour. 'Probably, we wouldn't have met at all, because my world is so far from yours.'

It was a fact. He knew he had no business making a commitment to anyone in his job. 'In fact, I've nothing to offer any woman.' The words came out involuntarily and his grip on her hand tightened. She was moving her fingers about slightly, caressing his.

'Well, I think you have,' she said softly, 'but you need to be more open.' She remembered how he'd been in complete control over the last few weeks, because he knew so much more than she did. She was realizing now, in affairs of the heart, she was much stronger. 'You shouldn't bottle things up.'

'I can't help it,' he said. 'I don't blame you for disliking me.'

'I never said I didn't like you.' She registered his cry for help, but she knew she couldn't do anything about it, until he told her the truth about Leila. Lucy couldn't imagine Conor being responsible for her death, but she needed to know.

She turned to him, safe in the knowledge he couldn't see her expression in the dark. She could feel the heat of his body next to hers. 'You just said you were telling me how you felt about me, in case we never got out,' she began.

'I shouldn't have said that.'

'It's all right. I know we might not,' she replied stoically. 'But, if something terrible is going to happen to us, I want you to know how I really feel about you as well.'

She felt him move nearer to her in the darkness. She warded him off.

'But, before I tell you, I want to know what happened between you and Leila.'

'Lucy, please.'

'No, you said you cared about me. If you do, you'll tell me. I can't bear it unless I know. How did Leila die?'

The silence that followed was very painful but, finally, Conor said, 'All right, but I warn you, it isn't a pretty story.'

'Go on,' she said, 'I'm waiting. I don't mind what it's like, as long as it's the truth.'

246

Chapter Eleven

'I was brought up in the Yemen, although I was educated at boarding school in England,' Conor began.

'My father was stationed in Aden with the colonial office and he and my mother struck up a friendship with Khalid's family. At that time, Khalid was a lecturer in Political Science and Philosophy at the University of Aden. Earlier on, he'd been head of one of the governorates, which replaced one of the statelets affiliated with his tribe.

'Abdul is Khalid's only son. Remember I told you he attended a minor public school in England?' Lucy nodded. 'It's quite usual for the sons of aristocratic Yemeni families to be sent abroad to be educated.

'Occasionally, he and I travelled home on the plane together and we'd see each other now and again in the holidays, but we were never very friendly. Most of his friends were young Yemenis. Even then he was anti-British.

'As for his sister, Leila,' he sighed, 'well, she was living at home. I fell for her, hook, line and sinker. She was lovely.' Lucy heard his voice falter and squeezed his hand to encourage him to continue. 'She'd been given an excellent education but, like most Yemeni girls, her destiny was an arranged marriage.

Khalid might have been westernized outwardly but he and Nadine still clung to the old tribal values.

'As I said, although Khalid's household was overtly westernized, he was still a stickler for convention and his wife and daughter used to be veiled in male company. I was never on my own with Leila and, although it seems hard to believe, I never even saw her face properly until a few years later.'

Conor was holding her hand very tightly now and Lucy was glad, because the story was taking shape in an entirely different way from what she'd expected. Somehow, she'd imagined Leila was some girl he'd met on his travels, like he'd met her.

'I'd have given anything to be alone with her. To cut a long story short, I was besotted with Leila and was dead keen on having her as a girl friend, but Khalid had already arranged a marriage for her.'

'Did he know how you felt about his daughter?' Lucy glanced across the dark room to where the unconscious Arab was lying.

'No, not in the beginning. Well, anyway, Leila went off and got married and I spent my time going backwards and forwards from Cambridge to Aden in the vacations. Sometimes, I heard about her from my parents. In fact, I made sure I did.

'By then, Khalid and Nadine were having a lot of trouble with Abdul. He'd got in with a fanatical crowd and I kept clear of him for the obvious reasons. I'd never liked the guy anyway.'

'I can understand that,' murmured Lucy, thinking of how crazy he'd looked when he pointed the gun at them, and how he'd shot his own father.

'Later on, the family was totally split when Abdul allied himself with a crackpot faction, which Khalid couldn't even countenance. Abdul went off to live in a training camp with them and he and his parents drifted further apart.'

'And what about Leila?'

'I'm coming to that,' he sighed. 'Unfortunately, she'd been married off to the aristocratic son of long-standing neighbors of Khalid's from his tribal village. This one. Of course, Khalid and Nadine found out too late, that her husband was tarred with the same brush as Abdul.

'She kept sending letters home telling them how desperately unhappy she was and, naturally, Nadine discussed it with my mother—they were very close—and the news filtered down to me. By then, I'd finished at university and was working as a civil servant in London.' Lucy considered the information the Foreign Office had given her about him. So, part of it was true.

'But I was never happy as a pen-pusher,' he continued, 'I wanted a bit more excitement in my life. I was transferred to the Yemen and, consequently, got myself involved with the Leila thing. Looking back, it wasn't a good move, seeing what happened.

'The long and the short of it was one day, I found myself going along with Nadine in her plan to fetch Leila home. In a country like the Yemen, getting a woman away from her husband amounts to kidnap.

'But Nadine was a very modern woman in some ways. A real fighter. Instead of abandoning her daughter, she thought she might be able to do something about the way she was being treated. I think Nadine saw me as a kind of saviour. I had influence, or she thought I had.

'We managed to find Leila, who was living a nomadic life under unimaginably bad conditions. It was worse in the Yemen for women then, than it is now.' Lucy found herself thinking what hell it must have been for the girl.

Conor added, 'She'd been through all kinds of terrible things like rape and abuse. She was a slave to her husband, who was as fanatical as her brother. She'd even been dragged round from camp to camp. She'd begged Abdul to help her when she met him, but like a lot of Yemeni men, he's not big on mercy. He still thinks all women should toe the line, and be kept on the straight and narrow.

'Well . . .' his voice was very low and Lucy

was straining to listen. '. . . as I told you, Nadine and I planned to get her out. I'd enlisted the help of several of my friends but, unfortunately, some of the villagers in the place where we were staying overnight betrayed us to Leila's husband.

'Both Nadine and Leila died when the house where they were sleeping was set on fire. Later on, we found out her husband set it alight on purpose.'

'Oh, no,' she said. 'How terrible. I'm so sorry.'

'I was in another house and got away unharmed. I had absolutely no chance of saving Leila and Nadine. I'm not proud of what happened there, Lucy. I don't want to go into the details, but, ever since then, this horrible anger has been burning away inside of me.' He lifted the hand, which was clasped in hers and placed it against his chest. She could feel the strong beat of his heart.

'It's been burning ever since at the injustice of the thing. That a man could get away with that kind of crime unpunished. Of course, Leila was branded as an adulteress because of my association with the kidnap, but she was entirely innocent. I'd never laid a finger on her.

'Nadine, who'd been a wonderful mother and wife, suffered the same fate all because of my involvement. Khalid lost his whole family on account of my stupidity. If I hadn't been

there, then maybe they'd both be alive today.'
Both he and Lucy sat in silence for a moment,
then he continued,

'I don't think I need to tell you what line
Abdul took. He accused me of having an affair
with his sister and luring her to her death,
although Khalid wrote to him several times
about the truth of it. Abdul believes what he's
always wanted to believe, that the West is
corrupt and Islam is holy.

'Afterwards, I left the Civil Service and
joined the Parachute Regiment.' He was silent
for a few moments then added, 'You wouldn't
have liked me if you'd known me at that time
of my life, Lucy. Although I've been a damn
good soldier and a fearsome enemy over the
last few years, I didn't have a heart. I was in
the Gulf War. I've seen it all, men at their best
and their worst.

'Joining the Special Forces was a natural
progression. I possessed everything they
wanted, the linguistic background and the
killer instinct. It was perfect. I've been all
over the world. Now, I'm here,' he finished
lamely.

'But, now, you've changed,' she murmured
softly. 'You have to forgive yourself. Leila's
death wasn't your fault. Nor was Nadine's. You
were trying to help them.'

'But I didn't succeed, did I?' He let go of
her hand.

'You can't always,' she said. 'Look how

you've protected me.'

'And look where it's got us.' He scrambled to his feet abruptly as if he couldn't bear sitting quietly any more.

Putting the sleeping Matt's head gently aside, she followed. Next moment, they were standing in the dark together.

'Conor,' she said softly, touching his back, 'listen to me. You did all you could do. That we've cnded up like this isn't your fault, any more than it was your fault Leila died. You were only trying to help.' Next moment, trying to comfort him, she was rubbing and massaging his shoulder gently with her small fingers. Very soon she could feel his taut muscles loosen under her touch. Then he was turning to her and a second later, she found herself in his arms.

She breathed a long sigh of relief as she cuddled close to him. 'Thank you for telling me about Leila,' she whispered. 'You wanted to know what I feel about you. About us? Well, I think we'll be okay together.'

'Do you?' She could feel his heart racing in his chest. Then she felt him searching for her lips. As his mouth sought hers, her whole body responded to the kiss. She wanted to stay like that for ever. To be able to imagine they were in some other place, where all the horrors of the last few days were quite forgotten.

She let him plant tiny kisses on her face and neck and tilting her head back, she savored his caresses. She clung to him dizzily, knowing if they never had the chance to go any further, they'd experienced, at least, one real moment of happiness, marred no longer by suspicion.

When he'd stopped kissing her, he whispered tenderly, 'If we do get out of this, I swear I'll do my best to—'

'Shhhh,' she said, placing a finger on his lips. 'Don't promise anything, please. I couldn't bear it, if I lost you.' He shook his head, not understanding.

'I thought that's what you wanted to hear,' he replied hoarsely. He had kissed plenty of women and, most of the time, it meant nothing. He'd never experienced the kind of feelings that were rushing through him now. The desire to protect her, to do everything for her, to love her and to save her life. All were encapsulated in that kiss.

'It's all right, Conor,' she said quietly. 'Only hold me, please.' He breathed in deep satisfaction as he felt her head nestle into the hollow at the nape of his neck.

They stood, pressed together in the dark, taking comfort from each other. Lucy was still very scared but being with him, made her feel safe.

She didn't know how long they'd been standing there when she heard Khalid groan.

'He's coming to again,' said Conor, breaking away. She followed him and the two of them bent over the injured Arab. He was trying to speak, but the words were unintelligible.

'Poor bloke,' Conor leaned back on his heels. 'If only we could have got him out, he might have had a chance.'

At that moment, they heard the bolt on the door slide back. Lucy looked across with frightened eyes, the moonlight illuminating her curly head, then back again at Conor.

'Chin up' he said, 'Just take your cue from me.' He glanced at his watch. 'Maybe they've wind of the choppers. Or Abdul wants us for something else.'

Seconds later, a torch beam was swivelling round the confined space, picking out Matt first, who was stirring, then on again to light up Khalid's motionless body. There it stayed.

Lucy's eyes were dazzled and her head started to go dizzy as the fresh air from outside flooded into their stuffy prison. Taking her cue from Conor, she scrambled to her feet and blinked up at their captors, fearing the worst.

Two of the men were holding rifles, while another two came quickly through the door, bent down and picked up Khalid, who cried out in pain.

Another gunman thrust through the narrow doorway and began to speak with Conor in rapid Arabic. Lucy only caught snatches of the conversation because she'd realized Matt had woken up. He cringed at the sight of the men, staring at them in terror. 'It's all right, Matt, it's all right. No one's going to hurt you,' she cried, rushing over to protect him.

Simultaneously, she saw one of the men put a finger to his lips. Conor hissed, 'Did you get any of that, Lucy? We're out of here. These men are loyal to Khalid. They're risking their lives to get us out, so keep your brother as quiet you can.'

'Okay.' Her heart was racing again as she tried to soothe Matt's fears. She felt broken-hearted, knowing instinctively that terrible things must have happened to him in that stuffy, little prison. The thought made her feel sick.

A moment later, she was following Conor, pulling her brother behind her into the open air. She didn't know whether he understood what was happening but, at least, he wasn't making any noise.

Then, suddenly, she felt Matt's legs begin to buckle. He almost fell, because she wasn't strong enough to support his weight on her own but, immediately, Conor was by her side and helping her.

Half-dragging Matt between them, and with the two Arabs swiftly carrying a moaning Khalid, they moved as fast as they could away from the village buildings, which stood black and menacing in the moonlight. All she was conscious of was the sound of cheering and singing in the houses behind her.

'They're celebrating because they think they've got it made,' said Conor grimly.

256

'Where are we headed?' she panted.

'Back to the hole. I have to get hold of the M10. Save your breath.'

It was the most heart-stopping journey Lucy had ever taken, even worse than when she'd entered the village that morning. Matt felt like a dead weight and her legs didn't feel like her own. She was parched and exhausted, but she strode blindly on across the plateau, telling herself to keep going, reminding herself it was only a quarter of a mile.

And, miraculously, no one was following them. No one knew they'd escaped and, before long, they were diving into the hollow. She and Matt lay there winded, not making a sound.

She watched silently as the four Arabs crowded around Khalid. One was bending listening to his chest, the other three sat back on their heels.

Meanwhile, Conor was hunched over the radio, the machine gun across his knees. It seemed years until he made contact. Then, with her hand rubbing her aching forehead and her heart in her mouth, Lucy heard him swiftly conveying the information. Minutes later, he joined her.

'How is he?' He indicated Matt. To her utter surprise, her brother replied weakly,

'I'm okay. Thanks to you.'

'Oh, Matt, you're back with us again,' she cried, trying to stem her tears.

'Can you use a pistol?' hissed Conor. Matt

nodded. Next moment, Conor was handing out one to both of them.

'What happens now?' she asked.

'We wait,' replied Conor. 'And hope Abdul doesn't find out we've escaped. If he doesn't, the most dangerous time for us will be when he hears the chopper and sends his men to fetch us. When they realize we've gone, we're going to have to hold them off.'

'But we've got them to help us,' retorted Lucy, looking at the Arabs. The one who'd been listening to Khalid's chest was now deep in conversation with the others.

'I doubt it,' replied Conor. 'All they're interested in is rescuing Khalid. They won't turn their guns on their own people.' His eyes narrowed as he watched them. 'I've a feeling Khalid hasn't made it. If so, they'll be off.'

'Do you think they'll betray us?'

'No, they'll want to put as much distance between themselves and Abdul as they can. He's not big on mercy.' Next moment, Conor was crawling over to them and listening to Khalid's chest himself. Then he looked across at Lucy and Matt, and shook his head.

'Oh, no,' said Lucy, turning to Matt. When she looked again, the last Arab was disappearing. Conor returned.

'Well, that's that. They're off.'

'Where have they gone?' asked Lucy.

'Down the mountain.' He stared across at Khalid. 'We've no time to bury him.' She shuddered, thinking about the young pilot. He looked at his watch. 'The chopper will be here in about fifteen minutes.'

'What do we do now?' whispered Matt, his voice still strangely cracked and his face haggard in the moonlight.

'We wait and we pray,' retorted Conor grimly. 'When you hear the engine, don't show yourselves until I tell you. By then, Abdul will have found out we're missing. It'll take a few minutes to search the village. Then he'll try the plateau and he won't be happy. Come on, Ali,' he breathed, looking at his watch again.

He glanced across at Khalid's body and sighed. Then he breathed in deeply. 'Well, I'll miss him. At one point, I thought he was going to turn on us, but he didn't let us down, after all. He was a good man. Pity it had to end like that. Now all the family's gone, except Abdul. Hopefully, that will be remedied soon.' His mouth was set and hard.

'What do you mean?'

'I mean Abdul's not going to get out of this alive.' Lucy stared up at Conor. All of a sudden, she thought she knew what his orders were.

'Do you mean you're going to kill him?' He didn't answer. He was inching himself to the top of the hollow. Matt and Lucy joined him. They could see torch lights flashing in the distance.

'They're on to us,' he said grimly. He looked up into the moonlit night. 'Come on, Ali. For Christ's sake, don't be late!' Simultaneously, they heard the throbbing of engines. 'Listen. They're coming,' he said. He smiled at Lucy and gripped her hand. 'And we have to hold on until they do.' The torch lights were also getting nearer.

He looked down at the machine gun and patted it. 'Yes, you beauty,' he said, 'I'm glad I brought you along.' Next moment, he was shouldering the heavy M10. 'Now keep back and don't fire unless I tell you to.'

Lucy and Matt crouched down together, holding their loaded pistols. She prayed mentally she wouldn't have to shoot anyone, but she knew that if she needed to she would. The roar of the approaching helicopters was getting louder by the minute, drowning out the shouts of the closing terrorists.

Then an enormous shaft of light was sweeping over the plateau, pin-pointing Abdul's men. Suddenly, gun fire merged with the engine noise and, as if in a dream, Lucy saw the men fall like skittles to the ground.

'Okay, they've got 'em!' roared Conor, 'get going!' Lucy and Matt struggled to climb up and out, with him pushing them from behind.

'Run like hell!' he shouted, 'Make for the chopper.'

As they ran, more and more choppers were arriving and landing, depositing bands of armed men, who stumbled out, then began to run towards the village. Conor was still behind them, pushing and urging them on the opposite way.

Then the chopper's great bulk was directly overhead and descending, the wind from its blades almost knocking them off their feet as it landed.

Lucy felt strong arms around her body, heaving her up. She stretched out her arms desperately and a man inside leaned out and grabbed her, hauling her into the chopper's deep belly. Seconds later, Matt was being pulled in beside her and, together, they collapsed onto the hard, steel floor.

Lucy struggled back to the edge as the helicopter took off. A soldier caught hold of her clothes and held on as she screamed, arms stretched out to him:

'Conor, Conor, come on!'

'I'm not coming with you!' he shouted back, cupping his hands to his mouth, 'Goodbye, Lucy. Don't worry, I'll see you. Don't—' The rest of his words were lost amongst the chattering sound of machine gun fire.

Then the chopper was fully airborne and she felt restraining hands pull her away from the open door.

She struggled free again to try and catch a last glimpse of him amongst the ant-like figures of soldiers streaming across the plateau. It was no use. She couldn't recognize him.

And, as the chopper turned away, flames were already leaping up from the village below.

'It looks like Hell,' she gasped.

'Never mind, Sis, we've made it,' Matt slurred, closing his eyes wearily.

But hers were fixed on the ever-diminishing flames. Somewhere, down there, in the middle of it all, was Conor, carrying out his orders.

Finally, when all she could see was the great, white face of the desert moon, she closed her eyes and listened to the noise of the engines, their rhythmical hammering keeping pace with her racing heart.

She told herself her brother was safe. She'd fulfilled her dream. They'd won, but the victory was all Conor's. The picture of him standing there, waving them off in the helicopter, was an image, indelibly printed on her mind. She remembered every little thing, his brave smile, the courageous set of his shoulders, the wind battering his clothes and the last words she'd heard from his lips, 'I'll see you.'

But would she ever see him again? She knew if she didn't, the world would never be the same.

When they were well underway, the chopper ran into some heavy air currents. As the night wind blowing off the mountains across the plain buffeted the helicopter unmercifully, she remembered what Conor said about the spirits, who walked on the wind.

Then Lucy gazed down into the darkness and prayed. *If you can hear me, please don't let anything happen to him. Please send him safe back home.*

*   *   *

Two hours later, they arrived at the camp where an Army doctor examined Matt and informed Lucy her brother was suffering from both malnutrition and dehydration which, coupled with the psychological problems of being for a hostage for so long, appeared to have sparked off the bizarre behaviour, which she'd been so worried about.

Thankfully, Lucy, herself, was pronounced fit and well except for a few cuts and bruises. After she'd seen Matt made comfortable and fixed up with a drip, she'd eaten a hasty meal and then the two of them were transferred to another chopper.

At the end of that journey, they were met by an official from the British Consulate accompanied by a doctor and nurse, who escorted Matt to a waiting ambulance. After seeing him off, Lucy was settled into a comfortable Land Rover with a blanket tucked around her knees and soon found herself following her brother on his way to hospital in Sana'a.

She leaned back wearily against the seat. Her head was aching alarmingly and she longed for bed, but her brain wouldn't stop going over everything that happened. Above all, she couldn't get Conor out of her mind. 'Do you know what happened back there?' she asked the official, desperate for news.

'I'm sorry, I don't, Miss Page,' he replied, smiling. 'But even if I did, I couldn't tell you. According to my information, the official line is that the hostage situation was resolved after Dr. Page was released by his captors. May I say, I think you've been very lucky.'

'So you don't know what happened to Conor Kendall? He saved our lives, you know.' She moistened her dry lips with her tongue.

'Afraid not. Guys like him, they just slip in and out. No one knows what happens to them. That's what they're paid for. Are you okay?' Her face was very pale.

'I'm a bit cold,' she said, drawing the blanket up around herself, thinking how monstrously unfair it all was, how she couldn't bear it if she never saw him again.

'I shouldn't worry, Miss Page,' remarked the official. 'I expect Kendall will turn up again like a bad penny. He always has before and, I'm sure this time will be no different.'

'I hope so too,' she said, staring miserably out through the window at the barren landscape. Then, as the Jeep bumped on, Lucy

264

lifted her eyes to look up at the navy-blue sky where, in the distance, the cold, red dawn was rising over the empty desert once more.

Chapter Twelve

The School of Oriental and African Studies in London was a gloomy place that afternoon in the middle of November, its grey, concrete walls only illuminated by countless lighted windows.

Lucy sat in her tiny office on the first floor, bent over an obscure historical tract, which she was translating from Arabic. Beside her lay one of her favourite cheese and tomato baguettes, laced with lettuce hearts and mayonnaise, which she'd fetched for lunch from the Refectory and from which she took the occasional bite.

But, she didn't have her mind on her work because, a few moments later, she decided moodily she still couldn't concentrate properly on anything. She'd felt exactly the same about her work ever since she'd returned from the Yemen, which seemed years ago now.

She walked slowly over to the window and stared out across the square to where a miserable plane tree, managing to grow from out of the courtyard tarmac, was ridding itself of its last few leaves, which were whirling about in the autumn wind. She hardly saw the tree, because she was thinking about past events again.

It had been the same ever since she'd returned to her job at SOAS. She couldn't explain to anybody quite what the matter with her was. She was sure her moodiness didn't stem from a desire to go back to the desert. It certainly wasn't because she yearned for excitement again. She knew she would never forget those terrible heart-stopping moments when her life was in danger. Fortunately, she didn't feel the irresistible pull of wild places like the men in her family.

She sighed again as she turned from the window and stared thoughtfully at her notice board, where she'd pinned her brother's photograph together with the press cuttings about his release. Matt's wan face stared back at her. He'd been in a bad way when they'd got him out but, now, he was fine. She was glad he seemed back to normal, although, privately, she wondered if he ever would be after what he'd been through.

However, his experiences as a hostage hadn't stopped him returning to the Yemen. Matt was his father's son and had gone back to his old job, lecturing in Archaeology at the University of Aden. It was like history repeating itself, although he promised Lucy and his distraught mother that he'd learned his lesson. Whether he'd keep his promise to stay out of trouble was another matter. That was up to him.

Lucy was happy all the hype was over. She hadn't enjoyed giving interviews because it brought everything back to her too cruelly. As she'd suspected, the first person to meet them off the plane was her old boyfriend, Nick. Although she could see he'd been hoping they would get back together now she was a personality, as he termed it, she'd given him short shrift.

She and Matt had been de-briefed as soon as they'd arrived and, subsequently, been warned not to speak of the assault on the terrorist camp, which meant she was forced to keep Conor's involvement a secret too.

Conor. His face came into sharp focus as it had done so many times since he'd waved good bye to her as she was swept away by the helicopter.

At first, she'd waited every day to hear from him. Every telephone call, every knock on the door had been an agony of suspense, but he'd never been on the other end of the line, nor standing on her doorstep. Months passed by and he hadn't made contact.

Lucy was almost sure now he didn't want to see her again. She'd gone over and over it in her mind. She told herself in his job he didn't have time to think about women. She remembered his bitter words, after he'd told her the story of Leila, 'I've nothing to offer any

267

woman.'

Sometimes, she was afraid he'd been killed in the assault, because she believed, if he'd survived, he would have got in touch with her. She'd asked the Foreign Office for information, but they wouldn't tell her a thing. If Conor was alive, then his movements were secret. She'd almost given up, but not quite, because she knew now she loved him. She'd been such a fool not to realize it earlier.

Lucy sat down at her desk and massaged her forehead. She realized feeling like this every day was doing her no good. She needed to move on and make a new life for herself. Her mother advised her to start doing all the things she'd been doing before her life was disrupted by the kidnap. One of those things was getting back with a persistent Nick.

But how could she have anything to do with him, when the only man she wanted was Conor Kendall? But there were no signs of much chance of a future with him. She sighed, consciously bringing herself back to the present with a jolt. This has to stop, she told herself. You have to move on. At least, you've still got a job you love.

That's how the counsellor advised her to think when she attended her last session. She'd been receiving counselling ever since they'd returned from the Yemen. Lucy hadn't been keen, but she'd gone along with it in the desperate hope it would help her with her feelings about being deserted by Conor, which was like bereavement. Whether counselling was doing any good, she didn't know, but she was persevering.

She took another bite of the baguette and stared at the mediaeval tract without interest. She'd told Kim the Chinese post-graduate researcher whom she shared the office with that she'd have the translation ready at the end of two weeks. Kim, with whom she shared a flat as well as an office, had gone to Hong Kong to see her parents and planned to be away for a fortnight.

Lucy didn't relish the thought of being all on her own, and was still trying to decide whether she should go and stay in Carshalton for a week to keep her mother company.

Trying to focus her mind on her work, she bent over her desk again but, a moment later, she looked up to see someone's shadow thrown on the upper frosted glass half of her door. The dim figure knocked.

'Yes? Who is it?'

'It's me,' replied a deep voice. Lucy frowned. She hadn't been expecting anyone. You could never be too careful these days.

'Who's me?'

'Conor.'

'What?' Lucy leapt up from the desk, ran to the door, grabbed the handle and was about to wrest it wide open, when she stopped. Taking a deep breath, she only opened it a crack.

It was Conor. Her first instinct was to throw herself into his arms, but she didn't. Instead, she stared at him as if she'd never seen him before, trying to commit every detail to her memory. He was wearing a moss-green roll-neck sweater and khaki Chinos, and he looked taller than she remembered.

'Lucy? How are you?' He stood there, awkwardly. He'd been wondering what his reception would be, ever since he'd made up his mind to see her again. His heart sank, thinking the worst. 'Can I come in?' he asked, his eyes searching her face hungrily.

She nodded, then took two steps back, put a hand to her mouth, turned from him, walked away, and flopped into the chair behind the desk. He felt at a loss as to what to say.

'How did you get past Reception?' It was a stupid remark, but her mind had gone blank.

'Easily,' he said. 'Your people here need to be careful about security. Anyone could get into this building. Should I have rung you first?'

'It might have been better,' she said. Lucy was afraid she was going to cry but then she controlled herself.

'I wanted to surprise you. Shouldn't I have?' He could see the tears starting in her eyes. 'Is something the matter?' He wasn't sure how he'd deal with tears. In fact, he'd been expecting her to be cross with him because he hadn't been in touch.

And she didn't disappoint him. Next moment, as she stared at him with those lovely, angry eyes, all the precious moments they'd shared came flooding into Conor's mind.

'Yes, the something is I haven't heard a word from you since . . . since you waved at me from that bloody helicopter. Now you turn up calmly asking me what the matter is. I thought you were dead. Where have you been?' He smiled in spite of his anxiety. So she was pleased to see him after all.

'I've been busy,' he said.

'Busy?' Her eyes narrowed. 'You could have phoned.'

'I couldn't.' He was walking over to the desk.

'It's November,' she said flatly.

'I know. Please don't think you haven't been on my mind. It's just . . .' he hesitated.

'You can't tell me where you've been, or what you've been doing. Okay, I get it, but it isn't fair. Anything could have happened to you.'

'Well, it hasn't,' he said. 'Come on,' he pleaded, 'Lucy, please.' Next moment, he came round the desk and squatted beside her swivel chair. Seconds later, his arms were round her. She let herself go limp, telling herself she ought to be able to behave rationally. She knew what his job entailed but, inside, his absence hurt like hell. Then she lifted her head, letting her curls brush his forehead.

'Don't be upset,' he said, smoothing back her hair with a gentle hand. 'I know you deserve an explanation, but it isn't easy.'

'It never is,' she sniffed, letting him go on caressing her. 'Can't you tell me anything you've been doing?' He wore a tender expression, as he looked into those agonized, blue eyes. She was even more beautiful than he remembered—and he remembered everything.

'You know I can't.'

'Oh, God,' she said hopelessly, 'is it always going to be like this?' She made to get up, but he wouldn't let her.

'No, it isn't,' he replied, brushing her hand with his lips. Her body burned at the light touch.

'What do you mean?' She didn't understand.

'I got myself a transfer. I'm out of it.' She stared at him in disbelief, and suddenly felt her anger melting away.

'You mean you've finished with Special Forces?'

'I hope I have.' She shook her head and closed her eyes in relief. She could feel his warm breath on her cheek.

'You never said you were glad to see me,' he breathed, head bent.

'Glad?' she said. 'I've never been happier in

272

my whole life.' She put up one hand and brushed away the tears from her cheek. With her other, she caressed his hair.

A moment later, they were entwined in a wordless embrace and kissing each other hungrily. When they stopped, he said, 'That's what kept me going these last few months, thinking about kissing you.'

'Was it?' Her voice cracked with emotion as her small hands stroked his face, his cheeks and his neck. It was then she felt the bumpy scar. 'What's this? What have you done?' She looked and saw the skin was white and puckered just above his collar bone.

'I haven't done anything. It was a slug from one of Abdul's men. It caught me in the neck. I suppose I can tell you I was in hospital for a bit, but it was no big deal.' He smiled. 'At least, it matches the other one.' She looked puzzled. 'The other one. On the back of my neck.'

'You mean the cross?' She felt embarrassed, remembering how she'd fantasized over how he'd got it.

'Yes, the one you were examining that first time when you were sitting behind me in the chopper.'

'But you had your back to me,' she cried indignantly.

'I know, but there was a mirror in the cockpit,' he replied, his eyes glinting in fun. 'I was waiting for you to ask me how I got it, but you didn't.'

'No,' she said, looking away from the scar. She couldn't bear to think about him suffering.

'Don't worry, this one only kept me down for a couple of weeks,' he said lightly. 'I won't go into details, except I was damned lucky it missed my jugular. Otherwise, I wouldn't have been here this afternoon.'

'Don't,' she said, the thought making her feel slightly sick. 'Anyway, how did you find me?' He smiled.

'Fancy asking me that. I knew where you worked. So I checked it out.'

'Well done,' she said ironically. Then she took his head in her hands and scrutinized his face. 'You look pale,' she said as if she was seeing him for the first time. 'And you've let your hair grow.' It was thick and curling over his collar.

'I was tired of being a skin head. New image. New man. You look great.'

'Thanks,' she smiled, straightening her blouse and looking down at her old Levis, 'but I'm a bit of a mess. I don't have to dress up for work.'

'I've seen you look a lot worse,' he quipped.

'Thanks for the compliment,' she retorted, but she knew what he meant. Then he was looking over at the notice board. He got up, walked over and stared at the press cuttings.

'How's it feel to be famous? '

'Not very nice actually,' she retorted.

'Where's that brother of yours?'

'I'm afraid he's back in Aden,' she grimaced. Conor lifted his eyebrows. 'But he's promised us, Mother and me, he won't get into trouble.'

'Has he now? Well, let's hope he means it,' he replied. his face suddenly somber. 'I wouldn't like you to go through all that again.' He walked away and over to the window, where she joined him.

'I wouldn't either,' she said, 'but I wouldn't be standing here now, if it hadn't been for you.'

'It was just a job,' he said quietly. They both stared at the bare plane tree.

'What are you going to do now?'

'That's up to you. Where shall we go?' he replied, misunderstanding. He saw her hesitate. 'If you want to.'

'Of course I do, but I meant, what will you do in the future?' She was hoping he was going to be asking her to be part of it.

'Oh, that.' He let out a deep breath and shrugged. 'Well, I'm still in the Army, but I'm attached to the Ministry. Whitehall.' He was frowning again.

'And you can't bear the thought of being a pen-pusher?' She didn't know whether she should be happy or disappointed. She couldn't imagine him anywhere else but in the desert.

'I don't mind pushing a pen,' he said, 'if I've other things to think about.'

'And what might they be?' She smiled back as he took her in his arms again and pushed

275

back another stray curly lock from her forehead.

'You,' he said, 'if you'll have me.'

'I will.' She nestled close to him, closing her eyes, savouring his nearness.

'What time do you finish here?' he asked softly.

'When I want.'

'What about now then?'

'There's nothing I'd like better,' she said, disengaging herself from his arms.

*   *   *

High in the London sky, the pale crescent of a new moon was far too weak to dispel the urban glow. Its wild companion, the autumn wind, drove the clouds across in flocks of orange then turned to leave its mark on the sleeping city, crazily shaking the red and gold leaves off the trees and whining round the houses.

In Lucy's bedroom, the curtains flew suddenly inwards. 'I'd better shut the window,' said Conor. They'd fallen asleep after making love, woken and made love again. Now their passion was spent and they were enjoying that easy familiarity, which comes to satisfied lovers. They'd also been reminiscing.

Her eyes lingered on his back, as he fastened the lock. 'Looks like a rough night,' he said, peering out into the dark street and up to the scudding clouds. 'And there's hardly any moon. Remember how we watched it in the desert?'

'How could I forget, after falling down that gully? Hurry up and come back to bed. I'm getting cold,' joked Lucy, as he turned towards her. Her eyes caressed his gorgeous naked body, which had given her more pleasure than she'd ever dreamed she could feel. She opened her arms and, seconds later, he was climbing in beside her again and they snuggled together.

She put her head on his chest. 'But, do you remember that sandstorm?' She looked up at the face she loved more than anything in the world. 'You know I was terrified.'

He stared down at her and gently stroked her silky skin. She almost purred under his touch. He laughed, 'I can remember something better than that.'

'You mean when we tried to make love in the cave?' He nodded, turning to her, letting his lips brush her face. She closed her eyes. 'I was such a little fool,' she added, 'thinking you didn't want me.'

'I wanted you from the very beginning,' he said. 'From the moment you saw that bullet proof vest.' He looked up to the ceiling, his eyes dancing with mischief.

'I hated wearing it.'

'You had such a horrified look on your face . . . and when I handed you that pistol—'

'I nearly died.'

277

'And you said you'd been taught how to use one at school.' He shook his head just thinking about it.

'I was a pain, wasn't I?' She giggled suddenly.

'No. I thought it was great how you took me on.' He considered for the umpteenth time how lucky he was she hadn't held his churlish behaviour against him. 'You know, after the crash, when I was trying to find if you had any broken bones, I nearly passed out after I made you take off your shirt.'

'Don't be silly,' she said.

'I did. You were so beautiful. I had to fight to keep my hands off you.'

'Did you?' she whispered. They went on playing their love games, going over all the times when they should have been truthful with each other and told each other how they really felt.

'And, finally, when we nearly made it, Khalid spoiled it all up for us,' he sighed.

'Poor Khalid,' she said.

'Yes,' he echoed. 'But, in the end, he did the right thing.'

'I don't want to think about anything horrible any more,' she said firmly, nestling close to him.

'Neither do I,' he replied comfortably. 'All that matters is, we got out safe and we're together. Are you happy, Lucy?'

'Very,' she said, closing her eyes and

nestling into his shoulder. Minutes later, he could hear her breathing become deep and regular as she slipped into satisfied sleep. Conor lay awake for a while, listening to the wind, his mind drifting aimlessly over the desert sands.

Then, suddenly, he yawned as sleep began to overtake him. 'Goodbye,' he murmured drowsily to the spirits he'd loved, who had been walking with him on the wind. He didn't need them any more. It was time they were laid to rest.